Child of the Snows

Child of the Snows

by

Thomas Besom

Golden Antelope Press
715 E. McPherson
Kirksville, Missouri 63501
2021

ISBN   978-1-952232-62-6

Library of Congress Control Number: 2021948110

Published by:
Golden Antelope Press
715 E. McPherson
Kirksville, Missouri 63501

Available at:
Golden Antelope Press
715 E. McPherson
Kirksville, Missouri, 63501
Phone: (660) 349-9832
http://www.goldenantelope.com
Email: ndelmoni@gmail.com

For my siblings
DG, Kim, and Beth

Contents

Child of the Snows

Chapter Illustrations

Cast of Characters

- **Amaru** ("snake" in Aymara): an older cousin of K'uchi-Wara.

- **Apu-Panaka**: state official whose job it was to select children for sacrifice.

- **Gerardo**: treasure hunter who found the mummy on Mount El Plomo.

- **Jaime**: treasure hunter who found the mummy on Mount El Plomo.

- **Jukumari** ("bear" in Aymara): K'uchi-Wara's cousin and friend.

- **K'uchi-Wara** ("happy star" in Aymara): main character, who was chosen for sacrifice by the Inkas.

- **K'uchi-Wara's Parents**: main character's mother and father.

- **Michimalonko**: chief of the Pecunche people in the Aconcagua and Mapocho Valleys of central Chile.

- **Nina** ("fire" in Aymara): K'uchi-Wara's girlfriend.

- **The Official**: state representative who accompanied K'uchi-Wara on his long trip south.

- **Old One**: senior priest who accompanied K'uchi-Wara on his long trip south.

- **Qispi** ("crystal" in Quechua): six-year-old boy from Chinchay-Suyu; he was K'uchi-Wara's friend and companion on the journey south.

- **Titi-Urqu** ("lead mountain" in Quechua; also called Cerro El Plomo in Spanish): sacred peak near whose summit a boy was sacrificed.

- **Vitacura**: Inka governor of the Aconcagua and Mapocho Valleys in central Chile.

- **Waman** ("falcon" in Quechua): junior priest who accompanied K'uchi-Wara on his long trip south.

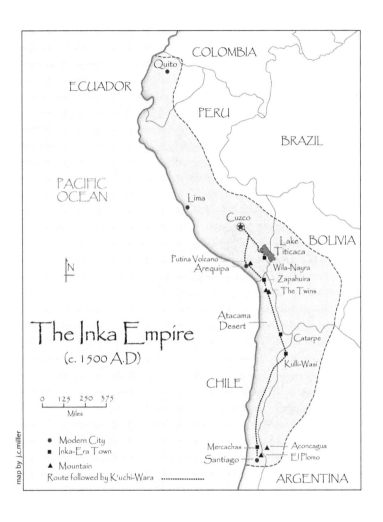

K'uchi-Wara's route across the Inka Empire

Prologue

The *Inkas*. The name conjures up images of a fabulously wealthy people, who had piles of gold and silver. It brings to mind a once mighty empire in South America, as well as Machu Picchu, an amazing citadel perched on a high mountain ridge.

Who were the Inkas? They were a native group who originally lived in the Cuzco Valley in what is today southeastern Peru. In the early fifteenth century, Pacha-Kuti, whose name means "transformer of the world," became their king. Under his leadership, they defeated various peoples around the valley, notably the Chanca. Thus they began to expand outward from their homeland and to create an empire. When the entire region was under their control, they turned their attention to Lake Titicaca. This lake, the largest on the continent, sits in a high basin on the border between Peru and Bolivia. Several powerful and prosperous ethnic groups occupied the basin, including the Lupaka. The wealth of the Lupaka lay principally in their vast herds of llamas and alpacas. The Inkas beat them on the battlefield and made their lands part of the realm.

Between 1463 and 1471, Pacha-Kuti ruled the empire with his son, Thupa Yapanqui. Thupa was a great conqueror. He took his armies north, where they won many victories. He added northwestern Peru and a large part of Ecuador to the quickly growing state. After Pacha-Kuti's death in 1471, Thupa went south. He led the Inkas against the Collagua, Cavana, Diaguita, Pecunche, and many other peoples, all of whom were defeated. He annexed southern Peru, western Bolivia, northern and central Chile, and northwestern Argentina.

Thupa Yapanqui passed away in 1493. Then the scarlet fringe that was worn on the forehead as a symbol of kingship, similar to a crown in Europe, went to Wayna Qhapaq. He acquired new lands in northern Peru and Ecuador. Under his leadership, the empire reached its greatest

7

size, stretching 2,500 miles from the Ancasmayo River that marks the present border between Colombia and Ecuador down to the Mapocho River in central Chile. The Inka capital, Cuzco, was located in the middle. Considering how big the realm was, unifying it was an amazing feat. Given that the Inkas incorporated so many different peoples into it, their achievement is even more impressive.

How did the Inkas unite their empire? For one thing, they built a far-reaching road system. By the early sixteenth century, their "royal highway" spanned almost 25,000 miles. It crossed wetlands, valleys, gorges, rivers, deserts, forests, and mountain passes over 16,000 feet high. It allowed the Inkas to march their armies throughout the realm to put down revolts. And it enabled goods, tribute and people to move between the provinces and the capital. Along the roads, the Inkas constructed *tampus*, lodging houses where royal officials could spend the night. Every half mile or so, they also built huts. At the huts, *chaskis* were stationed. The *chaskis* were runners who carried important messages for the state, and who operated as part of a relay system.

To better govern the realm, the Inkas established administrative centers throughout it. In what is today Chile, they built a string of such centers: Zapahuira, Catarpe, Mercachas, and Mapocho. They also made their subjects pay a special tax. But as they had no money, the tax, known as *mit'a*, was paid in the form of labor. The people worked on a rotating basis. They might serve in the army, or help construct roads, bridges and buildings, or till state fields. The Inkas also moved large groups of settlers from their native provinces to other parts of the empire. These settlers were called *mitmaq-kuna*. They were transplanted from regions that had been annexed for a long time to newly conquered lands, and vice versa. The reason for this shuffling of people was to break up rebellious groups and to spread Inka culture.

As every schoolchild knows, Christopher Columbus sailed to the New World in 1492. He was followed by explorers, soldiers of fortune, missionaries, treasure hunters, and colonists. Unfortunately they brought with them many diseases. King Wayna Qhapaq died from fever in 1525. Some historians think that he contracted either measles or smallpox, which were unknown in the Americas before the Europeans arrived. Forty years after Columbus's first voyage, Francisco Pizarro and a small army of 168 Spanish soldiers landed on the north coast of Peru. Thus began the Spanish Conquest. These men eventually brought down the Inka Empire. They also started the process by which the western part of South America was transformed into a colony of Spain.

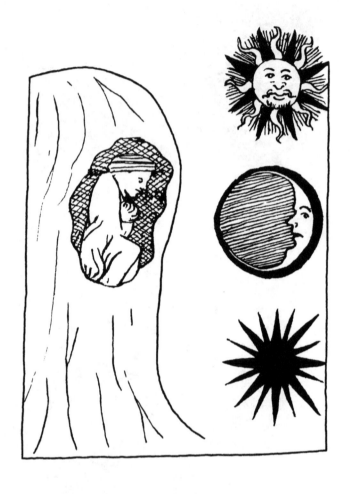

Child entombed within Cerro El Plomo (circa 1950)

Chapter One: The Discovery

Gerardo woke with a start. It was still dark. As he and Jaime were high on the mountain, he found it difficult to breath. He had spent the night inhaling through his mouth, and his throat was dry. He also had done a lot of tossing and turning. After reaching over to shake his companion, he started dressing. Given the burning cold and the fact they had no tent, he remained wrapped in his bedding while he dressed. It was no easy task. Putting on his sweater, thick pants, and two pairs of socks involved all sorts of contortions. He sat up and grabbed his coat. Wriggling into it was a struggle too. Then he stuck his feet into his boots, donned his woolen cap, and pulled on his gloves. As he stood and stretched, he let out a groan. His back was stiff from sleeping on the hard cold ground.

Breakfast was a simple and silent affair. Gerardo broke a hunk of stale bread in half. He handed one of the halves to Jaime, who took it with a gloved hand. Then Gerardo took out his pocket-knife and cut two wedges of cheese, one for each of them. They washed down the food with sugary tea. During the night, Gerardo had kept the liquid in a canteen next to his body so it wouldn't freeze.

They started their ascent. Moving in single file, with Gerardo leading, they worked their way up the slope. Overhead were thousands of stars, each a pin-prick of bright light. Ahead, where the bulk of the mountain blocked out the sky, there was only a black void.

Hour after hour, they trudged on. The going was tough. The moun-

11

tainside was steep and covered with loose rock, so for every two steps they took forward, they slid backward one step. As they walked, the rocks underfoot twisted and turned every-which-way, which meant they risked breaking an ankle. They tried to conserve energy by making their movements and breathing as mechanical and rhythmic as possible. Even so, they had to stop and rest often.

It was about 11:00 when they finally reached the main ridge at an altitude of 17,000 feet. Before them, situated on a stony knob overlooking the Iver Glacier, were the ruins of an ancient open-air temple. The temple was simple in design, little more than a circular platform measuring thirty feet across and five feet high. Its top was paved with flat stones.

"What d'you suppose it was used for?" asked Jaime.

"Don't rightly know," replied Gerardo. "Maybe the Indians carried out some sort of ritual here."

Jaime nodded.

Just beyond the temple, the slope dipped down to a spit of broken rock that jutted out into the middle of the glacier, a massive ice-sheet covering the upper part of the mountain. Gerardo and Jaime walked to the end of the spit, and gazed across the ice.

"Now what?" asked Jaime. "Where do we go from here?"

The stretch they had to traverse was not great, this being the narrowest part of the glacier. But the topmost section appeared to be steep. Finally Gerardo said, "We've no choice. If we want to find the mine, we've got to cross here." He stepped onto the ice. Jaime followed reluctantly.

Walking up the glacier was slow going. Although the ice was covered with crusty snow, there were patches that were very slippery. Gerardo thought back to an encounter he had had in the mountains many years ago. While out prospecting, he had run into a climber who spoke Spanish with a German accent. The man showed him the tools he used for climbing steep ice, which included sets of iron spikes that he attached to his boots. *We could sure use those spikes here. They'd make the going much easier. And safer!*

Up and up they went, Gerardo leading. At one point, he stepped over a narrow crack in the glacier. He looked deep into the blue-green ice and shuddered. *What if I fell in? We don't have a rope, so Jaime wouldn't be able to pull me out. I'd be stuck. And I'd slowly freeze to death.* Minutes later, he passed a field of ice pinnacles, each one as tall as a man. *How odd. They look like a parade of penitents during Holy Week.* He had seen photographs of such people as they marched through the streets of Spain in their high pointed hats and long white robes.

Gerardo grew weary. The greater his weariness, the less attention he paid to what he was doing. His body seemed to be on autopilot: stomp left boot into the hard-packed snow and inhale, stomp right boot into the hard-packed snow and exhale, stomp left boot.... His mind wandered. *I remember when I was little and would listen to Grandpa's stories. My favorite was the one about the Spaniard, who hundreds of years ago found a mine in the mountains around Santiago. The best part of the tale was Grandpa's description of the mine's richness. I can almost hear him say, "Gerardo, this mine had veins of pure silver. They were as fat as your arms, winding their way through crevices in the rock. All you had to do to get the metal was to whack it out with a pickax."*

But the end of the story always made me sad. Grandpa said the mine was secretly worked by a group of Indians. And when he'd get to the part where they stuck a knife in the Spaniard's heart to stop him from revealing their secret, I'd say, "No, Grandpa!" Worst of all, through time the mine's location was forgotten.

I was surprised, though, when later on I met that old geezer. He swore the story wasn't just a tall tale–that it was true! He claimed that the mine was on El Plomo's upper slopes! I wasn't sure that I should believe him. But here I am.

And now that I'm here, I wish I was somewhere else. I'd give anything to be walking through O'Higgins Park at this moment, shirtless and shoeless. I'd like to feel the warmth of the sun on my back, the tickle of the grass between my toes. I'd like to smell the roses that line the walkways. Their blooms should be fully open now. I'd like to hear the buzzing of the bees as they ...

That is when it happened. He slipped. Falling to the ice, he went sliding downslope, head first. He was on his back, arms flailing. He desperately tried to roll over onto his stomach, but could not. Faster and faster he went. He dug the heels of his boots into the slope, which did little to slow him down. He could feel rough ice tearing at his coat as he flew over it, could hear the whoosh of the air rushing past his head. Shooting by Jaime, he noted the look of horror frozen on the young man's face. He hit a steep section of glacier and began to pick up even more speed. Faster and faster he went. Then he slid over a bump and was momentarily airborne. *I'm going to die!* Suddenly his shoulder slammed into the hard-packed snow at the base of an ice pinnacle. He had stopped.

Gerardo slowly got to his feet. His heart was pounding and his shoulder ached. Someone was yelling something at him. Dazed, he looked around, then raised his eyes, squinting in the intense glare. *Where are my sunglasses? I must've dropped them.* He saw Jaime, who was now a ways uphill from him.

"ARE YOU OKAY?"

"Huh? What's that? Oh ... yeah ... I'm fine."

Gerardo had lost his canvas pack when he fell. Looking around for it, he was relieved to see that it too had come to rest at the foot of an ice pinnacle. Retrieving it, he swung it onto his back, and resumed his ascent. This time, he took care with each step. *What could we possibly find that would justify risking our lives like this?*

Reaching solid ground, Gerardo and Jaime dropped their heavy packs and flopped down. For fifteen minutes, they gasped and wheezed in the cold thin air. It was Gerardo, the more athletic of the two, who finally caught his breath. He got up to inspect their surroundings. They were on a broad plateau. Completely covered with fractured rock, it looked desolate. There were no plants, no animals. To their left, set against an impossibly blue sky, was an enormous rock, reddish-brown in color and shaped like a pyramid. In the distance, Gerardo made out range after range of snow-capped peaks. The scene was so awe-inspiring that snatches of the national anthem, only half remembered, played in his head:

> *How pure, Chile, is your blue sky,*
> *How pure the breezes that blow,*
> *Your flower-embroidered countryside,*
> *Is the happy image of Eden.*
> *Majestic is the white peak ...*

One mountain in particular caught his attention, it being considerably higher than the surrounding peaks. *It reminds me of a stallion, standing tall and erect. And look, there's a long white mane streaming off its summit ridge, which means there's a fierce wind blowing over there.*

Gerardo had wanted to find a silver mine on El Plomo's upper slopes. Instead his eyes settled on a rectangular structure, situated at the foot of the pyramid-shaped rock. It measured about twenty by ten feet. It was made of large irregular rocks, which some mysterious hand had gathered from a nearby pit, and had stacked to form nice straight walls. The structure was filled to the brim with soil. Gerardo could not see any soil in the vicinity, the ground underfoot being stony and frozen.

"What an incredible project," he muttered to himself, slowly shaking his head. *Just building this thing would've been hard enough work. But topping it off with dirt would've meant hauling hundreds of loads of the stuff up the mountain! And to think, I can barely carry my pack at this altitude. But who would've been crazy enough to take on a project like this? The Indians who lived here long ago?*

And what purpose did it serve? I don't know, but it must've meant an awful lot to someone. Otherwise why come to this God-forsaken place? Why make such neat walls when hardly anyone was ever going to see them? Why fill the structure with dirt? Is there something valuable hidden inside? Well, there's only one way to find out!

Gerardo went to his pack and pulled out a pickax. Returning to the structure, he clambered up onto its four-foot-high wall, stood, raised the heavy tool over his head, and brought it down with all his might. A cap of ice had formed over part of the soil. When the pickax struck it, an explosion of diamonds caught the afternoon light. The tiny chips of ice made a soft tinkling sound as they fell back to earth. Over and over, Gerardo drove the pickax into the ice until he broke through. By now he was completely winded and felt faint, so he slid off the wall, stuck his head between his knees, and panted. Jaime took over for him. He grabbed a shovel he had brought and set to work deepening the hole made by Gerardo. Pulling up shovelful after shovelful of soil, he saw pieces of dry grass, burnt wood, and cane in it.

Suddenly Jaime let out a yelp. "*¡CHITA!* Gerardo, look at this!"

Gerardo slowly got to his feet. Eyeing the top of the dirt pile, he saw a pair of figurines lying there. Examining them more closely, he realized they were stylized llamas. The first was red on one side and white on the other, and seemed to be carved from some kind of shell. The second figure was bright and shiny and yellowish in color. It was made of ... *gold*!

Fired up with excitement, Gerardo took over the digging. He kicked the blade of the tool as far as it would go into the earth. But when he removed a shovelful of the loose material, the walls of the cavity began to collapse. "Damn! The hole's too narrow," he said, glancing at Jaime. "I've got to widen it." That was quite the understatement because by the time his excavation was three feet deep, it was four feet across.

Gerardo was tiring again. He had just pulled up a shovelful of soil when something caught his eye. "What's that poking up out of the bottom of the hole?"

He knelt on the ice, took off his glove, reached down into the cavity, and brushed away the dry earth with his fingers. "Feathers? There are black and white feathers here." Jaime, who had sat down near their packs, could hear the bewilderment in his voice.

Gerardo replaced his glove. His fingers were already cold. He stuck his head and shoulders into the hole. Using his hands, he began scooping out dirt as carefully as possible. He exposed the plumes. They were followed by a head. As he continued digging, he uncovered a woolen mantle, hands, a tunic, and little feet wearing moccasins.

"*Dio' mío,*" he gasped. "My God! It's ... it's ... a *kid*!"

Gerardo lifted the small body out of the hole and brushed away the dirt that clung to it. Then he stared at it with open-mouthed astonishment. The remains were those of a child, curled up in a fetal position: legs crossed, arms wrapped around his knees, head resting on his breast. He was dressed in a black garment and grey mantle. Since his eyes were closed and his face serene, he looked as if he were taking a nap and might wake at any moment.

"JAIME, you won't believe this. *¡VEN PA'CA!* QUICK!"

Gerardo glanced at his companion, who had come up behind him. Then he returned his gaze to the child's face. It was painted red. There were diagonal yellow stripes that extended from the upper lip to the cheeks and from the nose to the eyes. Gerardo touched a cheek. It felt soft. This was strange since the body itself was as stiff as a board. Apparently it had been in the frozen ground for many years. He saw that the child's long hair, which was shiny, had been plaited into hundreds of little braids. The braids were partly obscured by a headdress consisting of a black band circling the crown from the back of which sprouted, like the long pointed leaves of an agave plant, feathers.

Questions swirled in the man's brain: *Who was this kid? Where did he come from? Who brought him up the mountain? He seems to have been sitting in the ground for a long time. But how long? Since before the Spanish came? Even more puzzling is why? Why go to so much trouble to bring him to such an out-of-the-way place? Why bury him? What did he do to be treated like this? Was he being punished? Or honored?*

K'uchi-Wara plays with the sling he received for his First Haircutting

Chapter Two: *Sutijara Kusisita Wara Wara* (Call Me K'uchi-Wara)

It was July. The two-year-old was standing with his parents in front of their house. With a chubby hand, he grasped his mother's long dress, which extended to her ankles. The guests started to arrive. They included friends and relatives, along with their families. As they passed him, he welcomed them with a phrase he had just learned: *"Suma jayp'u"* or "good evening" in Aymara. He stumbled over the words. The guests returned the greeting. One of his relatives tousled his long hair, to which he responded, "Don' do!" The guests sat down on the patio by the house. When all the invitees were there, the toddler's uncle, the eldest of his father's three brothers, formally welcomed them. He introduced the child too, who had little idea what was going on, but who smiled broadly. The boy was thrilled to be the center of attention.

The uncle picked up a ceramic cup filled with corn beer. He dipped his fingers into it, and sprinkled some of the liquid onto the two-year-old. He said, "A blessing on you." The boy squealed as the cold droplets hit his head. No one could tell whether he was squealing out of delight or distress. The uncle sprinkled the rest of the group with *chicha* too. In the distance were three snow-capped mountains. While the toddler looked on, his uncle honored each of them in turn. He took a mouthful of the thick brew, which he spewed toward it, being careful not to spit on the guests. He also poured some of the liquid onto the patio, and watched as it slowly seeped into the hard-packed soil. "A libation for you, Mother Earth." Then he set fire to a small pile of dried llama dung at the end of the earthen platform. He tossed offerings into it. The child made a face—eyes closed to mere slits, nose wrinkled, and lips puckered up—to show his disgust as the acrid smell of burning incense, coca leaves, and chunks of llama tallow reached him.

Once the offerings had been made, the uncle placed a colorful blanket woven from alpaca wool in the center of the patio. The boy's mother seated herself in the middle of it. The guests arranged themselves in two concentric rings around her, males in front, females in back. Meanwhile the toddler, who had lost interest in the proceedings, was wandering off. "I go play," he said. His uncle scooped him up and placed him in his mother's arms. But he did not want to be held. He squirmed in an effort to escape until she told him, "Sit still." The uncle grabbed a bronze knife, whose blade had been given a fine edge. He cut hanks of hair from his nephew's head, collecting them in the palm of his hand and depositing them in a ceramic bowl. When the uncle was finished, the two-year-old ran his hand over his head. It looked like a harvested field. His eyes grew large as he discovered there was nothing left but stubble. As surprise turned to dismay, he began to wail. "Hush," his mother scolded.

The uncle trimmed his nephew's fingernails too, being careful to collect the clippings in the bowl. He emptied the contents of the vessel into a leather pouch, which he gave to the mother. Thinking that this would be a good opportunity to teach the younger guests about Lupaka beliefs, he said: "In the future, whenever the child's hair is cut, his nails are trimmed, or he loses a baby tooth, all the bodily refuse will be saved for him. Why do we do this? What purpose does it serve?"

"Well," said a boy, who was watching intently, but who wasn't very sure of himself, "don't ... don't we do it so the person's spirit can rest in peace?"

"That's right," the man replied encouragingly. "What would happen if we didn't save all the little bits and pieces of a person's body for him?"

"I know, I know," a girl answered. "After he died, his spirit might get restless and go looking for them!"

"Very good."

The girl beamed.

The uncle returned his attention to the toddler, still fidgeting in his mother's lap. Facing the child, and adopting a formal tone, he said, "From now on, you'll be known as Kusisita Wara Wara ('happy star'). But that's a lot to say. So we'll just call you K'uchi-Wara." His announcement was greeted with nods of approval from the older guests. As he loved making speeches, and had put a lot of time and thought into this one, he continued. "As you know, each thing on earth has its twin in the sky. And the celestial body is responsible for the well-being of its counterpart in this world. So we honor the Great Llama because the constellation keeps our herds healthy and fertile. That being the case, why shouldn't there be a star connected with human happiness? By naming my nephew K'uchi-Wara, I hope his celestial twin will smile on him always. And will grant him long life and prosperity!" The guests cheered.

"As you also know, the name has a second meaning, which is 'something to be admired.' It's my sincere wish that when the boy grows up, others will look up to him. That he'll be a man whom all the Lupaka can be proud of!" With these words, the uncle took his cup of corn beer and drank. Then he handed the vessel to K'uchi-Wara's mother so she could drink.

The high point of K'uchi-Wara's First Haircutting, at least for the toddler, came when everyone presented him with gifts. His uncle boasted, "I'm giving my godchild a pair of alpacas, a male and a female. Like the boy, they've recently been weaned." Then, to instruct the children present on Lupaka tradition, he added, "The animals will make up the core of K'uchi-Wara's personal herd. It will grow through time. Eventually it will become big enough to support a wife and family."

Many guests followed suit. K'uchi-Wara was from a noble family, his father being the village headman, so his kin could afford to spoil him.

Some relatives told him that they too would contribute animals to his personal herd. People from less well-to-do families gave him clothing of alpaca wool, or miniature farm tools to play with. Lastly his uncle handed him a small sling of braided llama fleece. Accepting it with chubby hands, K'uchi-Wara's eyes lit up. He said, "*Yus ... yuspagara–* thank you." He was so thrilled with the sling that for the rest of the evening he refused to put it down. He paraded around with it, smiling and showing it off to all the guests. They nodded and told him how lucky he was to receive such a nice gift.

The low point of the evening came when his mother caught him swatting the dog with the sling. "Stop that right now," she scolded, "or I'll take it away from you."

K'uchi-Wara's mother had spent much of the previous week in the kitchen. Now she, together with her female kin, served a special meal. They hauled out a large ceramic pot that was brimming with thick stew. It was made from llama meat, potatoes, and assorted greens. It was seasoned with chili peppers and salt. While the mother ladled the stew into serving bowls, an old aunt distributed the steaming bowls to their guests on the patio. The males sat together on one side, the females on the other. While some ate the viscous dish with their fingers, others scooped it up with *quinua* bread. K'uchi-Wara was famished. As soon as the ancient woman set a bowl in front of him, he stuck his face into it and slurped up the stew. By the time he was finished, his head, hands, and the front of his tunic were filthy. "Honestly!" his mother muttered when she saw him. "Sometimes I think you're more trouble than you're worth." She got a cloth from the kitchen, dampened it, and cleaned him up as best she could.

The women served a thin broth for the final course. When the guests had eaten their fill, they patted their bellies. Some of the men let out a loud burp. Everyone agreed it had been a great meal.

The festivities did not end with dinner. As the sun sank toward the horizon, the boy's uncle appeared with a massive earthenware jug, which he set down on the patio. Then he said, "I have a real treat for all of you!

In May, after a lot of negotiating, I was able to secure a fair quantity of corn from relatives who live on the Kotakawana Peninsula. In June, the young women of our community got together to chew the corn. They had to spend several days at the task." For the children's benefit he added, "During the time that they chewed, they had to avoid eating salt and chili peppers.

"Well, for the past month the corn's been fermenting. And as the resulting *chicha* has steadily matured, it's gotten thicker and stronger. Now it's ready to drink!" The adults cheered.

K'uchi-Wara's mother walked among the guests, handing out wooden cups. She was followed by a female relative, who carried a ceramic vessel with a rotund body, pointed base, and long neck. The woman used this vessel to fill the cups.

The boy's father sat down on a low stool at the far end of the patio. He wore the trappings of his office as a Lupaka headman: a fine tunic, a black band that bound his shoulder-length hair, a silver pendant shaped like a double crescent that dangled under his chin, a wide silver bracelet that circled his right wrist, and llama-hide moccasins that covered his feet. In his hand was a delicate wooden beaker nearly overflowing with corn beer. He raised the beaker and said, "I toast the mummies of my ancestors, nestled in their towers of stone. They are not only the foundation of my bloodline, but the links that tie me to the dawn of time. *They* are the past." He drank deeply. Everyone followed suit.

He continued: "I toast the three mountains we see before us, bathed in the ruddy glow of the setting sun. As our gods, they protect us from harm, sustain us with life-giving water, make our herds fertile. These *peaks* are our present." He drank deeply. Everyone followed suit.

Then the father said, looking directly at K'uchi-Wara, "I toast my only child, who today celebrates his First Haircutting. He's the one who'll take my place as headman when I'm gone. He's the next link in the unbroken chain of my lineage. *He* is the future!" As he raised the wet beaker to his lips to take another swallow of corn beer, though, the vessel slipped from his fingers. It fell to the floor, smashing to pieces.

"Oh, no!" an old woman wailed.

"What is it?" K'uchi-Wara's mother asked. "What's wrong, grand-mother?"

"Don't you know? In my day, a botched toast was considered a bad omen. Especially if it happened during a First Haircutting! This doesn't bode well for the boy."

"Nonsense. That's just superstition."

"Superstition? You think I'm superstitious?" the crone sputtered. "You heed my words, the child's life will be marked by sorrow!"

Despite the interruption, the drinking continued. K'uchi-Wara's moth-er and her kinswoman had to scramble to refill each person's cup.

After the drinking had gone on for a while, an old man stood up. He was unsteady on his feet. He shouted, "Let's have a song! All of you know 'Chambi' ('he who brings good news'), don't you?" And he began to sing:

> Walking with his llama,
> His cloth bag full of *chuño* (dried potatoes),
> Chambi travels to a fiesta,
> Where the bright skirts whirl.
>
> After walking for a time,
> Chambi sleeps beneath a tree.
> But during his short nap,
> His llama eats his grub.
>
> As Chambi wakes from sleep,
> He finds his food is gone.
> "What've you done, my pet?
> Now my belly won't be full."
>
> When Chambi hits the fair,
> He tries the local beer.
> He bids his llama, "Drink,
> So our hunger we'll forget!"

> They've both had many cups,
> They're both completely drunk.
> Returning to their town,
> They dance along the path.

K'uchi-Wara's father, as well as every other man, always carried a *ch'uspa* containing coca leaves. This small cloth bag had a long strap that he slung over one shoulder and across his chest so it hung at waist level. Turning to his brother, the father offered him unbroken leaves that he had carefully chosen. They were oval in shape, with tapered ends. The brother took them and returned the favor. The other men on the platform likewise exchanged coca.

The father then presented his wife with some perfect leaves. "*Yuspagara*," she said, accepting them with both hands. The rest of the women received coca too. Soon every adult had a lump in his or her cheek consisting of a wad of leaves—slowly being chewed with a pinch of ground quicklime. As the juices from the coca flowed and mixed with the lime, the people's mouths and tongues were numbed, and they felt energized. The celebration became livelier.

K'uchi-Wara was curious about the little green leaves. He went up to his mother and tugged on her dress. He pointed to a leaf in her hand, then to his mouth.

"What? You want to try coca? Is that it?"

He nodded.

She smiled. "I'm sorry, son, but you're much too young. You'll have to wait till you're older. Besides, you wouldn't like them. They're very bitter."

Night was falling. The mother went into her house and brought out some lamps. She lit the wicks, which were set into bowls of llama tallow, and placed them around the patio. They cast a warm light, but weren't really needed. When the sun had set, a nearly full moon had risen, illuminating the guests, the platform, the homestead, the whole mountain slope. In the distance, the three snow-capped peaks seemed to glow as if lit by an internal source.

K'uchi-Wara's father had invited a group of musicians to the First Haircutting. They arrived with an assortment of instruments. There were various sized flutes, panpipes, and drums. There also were bells and rattles. When the band began to play, people leapt to their feet to sing and dance. Husbands took their wives' hands, young men grabbed their sweethearts, and soon the patio was crowded with whirling couples, including the toddler's parents. Around and around they went. "What a lovely night," the mother murmured into her husband's ear as she caught a glimpse of the moonlit mountains. "But I keep thinking about what the old woman said ... about our son's future."

"Don't worry about it. She shouldn't have said those things. I think K'uchi-Wara's First Haircutting has been a great success, which means his future will be bright!"

"I hope so."

Off to the side of the patio, K'uchi-Wara and his cousins, all of whom were young, danced. Or they tried to: they clapped their hands, stomped their feet, and moved to the beat as best they could. What they lacked in grace, they made up for in enthusiasm.

The guests performed line dances, circle dances, dances for men, and dances only for women. Although the music continued late into the night, K'uchi-Wara's energy flagged. When his mother first noticed him slowing down, she suggested he go to bed. Instead he threw a tantrum. "I don' wanna sleep!" he said, stamping his foot on the ground.

Before long, however, he gave a wide yawn and rubbed his eyes with the back of his hand. Then his head began to slump. He offered no resistance when she picked him up and carried him into the house, where she laid him on the family's sleeping platform, located against the back wall. The platform was of adobe and should have been uncomfortably hard. Even so, the child didn't mind sleeping on it. In fact, he loved the cushy mattress, which was made of highland grasses tied into thick bundles. His mother drew a large blanket of soft alpaca wool over his body and gently caressed his cheek. "You've had quite the day. Good night."

The last thing K'uchi-Wara was conscious of, as he clutched the sling tightly to his breast and drifted off to sleep, was the sound of panpipes and of feet shuffling across the compact earth.

K'uchi-Wara dreams he is a condor flying over his homeland

Chapter Three: The Dream

K'uchi-Wara sat up. He swept shoulder-length locks from his face. Then he rubbed the sleep from his dark brown eyes. He was alone on the sleeping platform, his mother and father having risen earlier. It was still dark in the cottage. But he could see dusky light coming through the space between the door, llama hides stretched over a wooden frame, and the doorjambs.

K'uchi-Wara had had a dream the previous night that he replayed in his mind. *That was no ordinary dream. It was so intense, so incredibly real.* He had been a mighty condor with a black body, wings that were as long as a man is tall, and a white collar around his neck. While soaring through the great expanse of blue, he had heard the smooth flow of air over his feathers, and had felt the warmth of the sunshine on his head.

When he looked up, he saw Inti, the Sun, shining in all his glory. In the distance were the three snowy peaks that his people considered sacred. The middle one, the highest, was called Qala-Uta. *Your name really suits you, Qala-Uta, since you're made of stone, and have a blocky shape like a house.*

Spread out below was the whole world as he knew it. There was the long gentle slope where the members of his community lived. There on a flat space in the middle of the slope was the homestead belonging to his extended family. With his keen vision, he saw every detail of it: the four rectangular cottages occupied by his household and by those of his father's three brothers. The cottages were loosely clustered around a patio. Attached to each of them was a square room, the kitchen. The buildings had gabled roofs thatched with *ichu* grass, which grew wild in the area. He spied four oval rock walls that defined potato gardens, one for each household. There also were seven large rectangular corrals, and a small circular corral. Within the corrals were specks of black, brown, white, reddish-brown, and grey, the extended family's llamas and alpacas.

A footpath that looked like a thin ribbon ran from his homestead to another one across the wide ridge. As he looked up and down the slope, he could make out other family homesteads, which were somewhat evenly spaced, and connected by similar footpaths. Between them were piles of glacier-crushed rock and expanses of *ichu*. K'uchi-Wara swelled with pride at the sight of Wila-Nayra, and at the thought that he was the son of the village headman!

In his dream, the boy-condor continued following the contours of the land as it steepened above Wila-Nayra. From his high vantage point, the slope, covered with clumps of tall feathery grasses and with a rocky spine running down the middle of it, resembled the broad and hairy back of a giant. Alongside the giant's spine was a trail. It led upward for several hundred vertical feet to a flat space, where there were several pools. They were the "eyes" of the peak. Spying one that was a vivid red, K'uchi-Wara swooped down for a closer look. He had the unnerving sensation that his stomach was in free fall. "WHOOOOA," he yelled. The pool was also called Wila-Nayra. It was so distinct, it had given its name to the community below. As the great bird circled it, he dipped a wing in its shallow waters. "*Ayayau*–ouch! That's hot!" Covering the bottom of it, he could see a slimy film the color of blood. *The other "eyes" are cold, while Wila-Nayra's hot. And this pool's the only one that's red. Why would that be?*

Then K'uchi-Wara glided along the footpath as it zigzagged up an even steeper incline to a pass. Nearing it, he spread his wings wide and caught an updraft that shot him high into the sky. "WHEEEE." Peering down from the blue, he saw a level space with a dozen circular towers. His father had taken him to see these *chullpas* several times. So he knew from personal experience they were as high as two men, one standing on the other's shoulders. They were as big around as the ring formed by six people with joined hands. They had straight walls and domed tops. Landing beside one of them, he hopped to its door and peeked inside. The interior chamber, lit by the morning sun, had nice smooth walls plastered with adobe. It was crowded with the mummies of his ancestors. The cold dry air that had desiccated their faces and bodies had also preserved their colorful garments and feathered headdresses. K'uchi-Wara greeted them. "Maybe someday," he told them, "I'll join you."

On the far side of the pass, the condor sighted additional pastures used by his community. *It's a good thing we have so much grazing land, and can scatter our llamas and alpacas all over it. Otherwise they'd be bunched together and would quickly eat all the grass. Then they'd starve. And so would we.*

K'uchi-Wara had visited these more distant pastures, but had never gone beyond them. Now he sailed over the imaginary line marking the boundary between his universe, everything he had seen and experienced in his eight years, and the unknown. Doing so, he began to grow. Soon he was as big as a mountain and could fly faster and higher than ever before. With wings extended—the wind surging over and under them, giving him enough lift to keep his huge body aloft—he headed toward the east. Before long he was soaring past a huge turquoise-colored lake sitting in the middle of a high basin. *That must be Lake Titicaca.* Subsequently he was over the Andes Mountains, the backbone of the South American continent. There were rows and rows of peaks, which formed an army standing at rigid attention. The warriors were clad in heavy armor of ice. On their crowns they wore helmets of dazzling white. Looking at them was bad enough, but doing so while heading toward the sun was blinding. So K'uchi-Wara changed course and started flying in a more northerly direction.

As he left the mountains behind, the land flattened out and turned more verdant. Green, green, green, as far as the eye could see! Occasionally the monotony of the landscape was broken by the silver shimmer of a river. As K'uchi-Wara gazed at the emerald canopy, he discovered with his magical condor eyes that just beneath it was a kaleidoscope of life and color. There were macaws decked out in brilliant plumage of scarlet, blue, and yellow. There were sleek black monkeys hanging lazily by their tails. There were giant anteaters with pointed snouts, long pink tongues, and bushy brown tails. And there were elegant jaguars, whose golden coats were stamped with black rosettes.

Then K'uchi-Wara was flying over an endless expanse of blue water. *Is that Mama-Kuta below?* All at once, the boy-condor spied three objects bobbing on the waves. He glided down to inspect them. *How strange! They seem to be floating houses made of wood.* Each one had three large poles rising from its deck to which were attached enormous pieces of white cloth that billowed in the wind. Some of the pieces of cloth were painted with red crosses. There were strange men on the decks too. When they spotted him, they gawked and pointed. A man raised a long stick and pointed it at him. He heard a BANG, and was startled awake.

K'uchi-Wara practices with his sling during a typical day

Chapter Four: One Day in the Life

Bounding from the sleeping platform, K'uchi-Wara, who was already wearing a tunic, grabbed his grey mantle from a wooden peg sticking out of the wall. He wrapped it around his shoulders and went out the door. He was shoeless, even though the ground was covered with frost. But as he rarely wore moccasins, his feet were calloused and tough. The pallid sun had just cleared the mountain ridge to the east. It shone down onto the collection of buildings, casting long shadows, and making the ice crystals glitter. The boy's father was standing on the patio talking with the uncle who six years earlier had cut K'uchi-Wara's hair for the first time. Going up to the men, the child greeted them.

"Well, well. Look who decided to make an appearance this morning. Go see if breakfast's ready," his father said.

There was no door connecting the house directly to the kitchen, so the boy scampered around to the back of the building. He stopped to pee along the way. Taking aim at a thick patch of frost—psssss—he melted a wide hole in it. He watched with glee as the liquid soaked into the earth, leaving a dark stain from which small puffs of steam rose.

Reaching the attached room that served as a kitchen, he entered. But he left the door ajar.

"*Shut* the door!" his mother commanded. "It's cold outside. One would think you were raised in a llama corral."

"Sorry," the boy said, rolling his eyes. He did as he was bid, though.

"Dad wants to know when we'll be eating."

"Just a little while."

Rather than telling his father, K'uchi-Wara sat on the hard-packed earth, and drew his tunic down over his knees. Beside him was a rectangular hole that had been dug into the kitchen floor. The hole's flat bottom was covered with grass. Movement inside it caught the child's attention. He reached in and picked up a guinea pig. The animal, brown with white spots, was one of a half-dozen guinea pigs that they kept in the kitchen. Holding the critter's face next to his own, he looked it straight in the eye. He opened his mouth wide as if he were going to devour it. It began to shake, and let out a series of high-pitched squeaks. Then the eight-year-old laughed. He gave the animal a pat, and returned it to the hole.

"Can we have guinea pig for dinner?"

"Those animals aren't for us, dear. We're fattening them up for sacrifice to Qala-Uta."

"Why does the mountain get them?"

"He's our father, a part of the family. We live together and share food. He provides us with alpacas and potatoes, we give him guinea pigs and llama fat."

"Oh."

"Speaking of guinea pigs, would you feed them?"

"Oh, Mom, I always have to do everything!"

"Yeah, we work you to death, don't we."

Set into three walls of the kitchen were niches, where the boy's father had placed ceramic vessels of various sizes. They held water, *chicha*, grain, and salt. Stacked against the fourth wall were rough woolen sacks containing various dried products: potatoes, coca leaves, llama and alpaca meat, some corn, and chili peppers. The child stood up, went over to a large earthenware pot, and stuck his hand in. Pulling out a fistful of *quinua* seeds, he scattered them among the guinea pigs.

"Was that *really* so hard?" said his mother.

"I guess not."

"Complaining about doing a simple chore usually takes far more effort than actually doing it."

K'uchi-Wara plopped himself down so he could watch his mother cook. He liked to see how she went about it. She stood before her pottery stove, in whose front was a large oval hole. Peering into the hole, she made sure the dried llama dung was burning evenly. Atop the stove sat two ceramic pots. The boy could hear their contents bubbling, could see steam rising from them. When his mother stuck a wooden ladle into the larger pot and stirred, a rich and savory aroma wafted through the room. The boy thought he recognized the smell. Even so, he asked, "What's for breakfast?"

"We're having soup made from an alpaca shank and *quinua*. Also boiled red potatoes."

"Not again! We had that the other day."

"Stop your whining! I've had enough of it, and the day's just begun. I got up before dawn to start breakfast so it would be ready by the time you got out of bed. If you don't like what I'm fixing, you can make your own food. Or go hungry."

"I was just *saying* ... I didn't mean anything ..."

"You don't know how lucky you are. There are food shortages in Cavana! I'm sure plenty of children in *that* province would be thrilled to get alpaca-shank soup for breakfast."

K'uchi-Wara said nothing. He watched as white smoke from the dung fire slowly drifted upward, wreathing around the framework of wooden poles that supported the thatched roof. Large bundles of dry *ichu* grass had been bound together with rope and lashed to the poles. When the smoke hit the underside of these dense bundles, it flattened out before slowly filtering through them.

"Mom?"

"Yes?"

"Why don't you give me a baby brother?"

"Because some days you're more than enough for me to handle."

"What do you mean?"

"What do I mean? Just this: if we didn't need your help with the herding, we'd probably give you away to the Inkas," she said with a wan smile. "I'm sure they could put you to good use."

"Mom?"

"*Enough* with the questions. Breakfast's ready. Go get your father."

The family ate on the patio. When the meal ended, K'uchi-Wara was sent to meet his cousin, Jukumari ("bear"). About the same age as K'uchi-Wara, Jukumari had been given the name because he was burly, barrel-chested, and lumbering, like a bear. As he lived in one of the four cottages grouped around the patio, K'uchi-Wara did not have far to go to find him.

"We're supposed to take eighty alpacas to a high meadow to graze," K'uchi-Wara told his cousin. "I'm also going to take the four females and two geldings in my personal herd. You can take the animals you received for your First Haircutting, if you want."

Jukumari simply said, "Okay."

The cousins entered a rectangular corral, where the shaggy beasts were still asleep, seated on the ground. Their legs were tucked under their bodies for warmth. "CH', CH'UY, CH'UY!" the boys yelled. "CH', CH'UY, CH'UY!" The alpacas immediately opened their eyes. They awkwardly staggered to their feet. Then the boys went into the neighboring corral and roused its occupants. The animals in the two enclosures, which were but a fraction of the extended family's herd, were all females and geldings. K'uchi-Wara's father, while in his "teaching mode," had explained to the child that, "males can be aggressive and difficult to control, so you should castrate them when they're three years old. You only need a few non-geldings for breeding."

K'uchi-Wara and Jukumari led the herd of alpacas up the mountain slope to the level area where the "eyes" were located. There they let their charges drink. But they had to shoo some of the animals away from the pool called Wila-Nayra as it was sacred.

While dangling their bare feet in one of the cold-water "eyes," Jukumari said, "Ahhh, this is the life."

"I'll say!" Then K'uchi-Wara became more pensive. He looked over at his cousin. "I had a strange dream last night."

"Oh?"

"Yeah, I dreamt that I was a giant condor, flying over our lands. Then I went past Lake Titicaca, through the mountains, above a huge jungle, and over the ocean. The odd thing is that while I was going over Mother Sea, I saw a house floating on the water. What do you make of it?"

"Well, condors fly between heaven and earth. So they mediate between the gods and us. Maybe one day you'll have something to do with the gods. But you say that you saw a floating house? Was anyone in it?"

"Yeah, there were men on top of it. They were tall, I think, with pale skin."

"Sounds like Wira-Qucha and his sons! Maybe it means that the Creator will be returning to us from across the sea. Maybe you're going to help him in some way."

"Hmm," said K'uchi-Wara, not entirely convinced. Then he fell silent. He gazed down into the pool, where they still dangled their feet. As the water was exceptionally clear, he could see that its sides were funnel shaped. At the bottom was a hole no wider than his foot. "Speaking of Wira-Qucha, remember the legend that Uncle told us the other night? The one about Creation. And about how the first ancestors left the center of the mountain and came out into this world by way of the 'eyes.'"

"Sure. What about it?"

"Do you think the legend's true?"

"I guess so."

"Then how come the ancestors didn't drown when they swam up through the pool?"

"How should I know? Maybe they were good at holding their breath."

"Okay, then why didn't they get stuck in that tiny hole down there?"

"Um ... because ... they were ... skinny?"

"You've seen the mummies of our ancestors in their *chullpas*. They don't look any skinnier than our parents. And I don't think my dad could fit through there."

"Good point. So what are you saying?"

"Maybe Uncle was teasing us. Maybe the story isn't true, and he just wanted to see if he could fool us."

"But," Jukumari protested, "my parents told me the legend's important to our community. It tells us how we got here. And why this land belongs to us."

The alpacas, having drunk their fill, left the pools. Following the lead animal, they slowly made their way along the slope, munching on tall grasses as they went. All the while they "hummed"—made a closed-mouth droning sound, something like a purr—to show their contentment. K'uchi-Wara grabbed his cousin's arm. "Jukumari, the animals are heading for that meadow over there. Let's get ahead of them. Then, while we wait for them to catch up, we can practice with our slings!"

"Good ide ..." Jukumari started to say, before he realized that K'uchi-Wara was already sprinting away from him. "HEY, WAIT FOR ME," he yelled, and took off in hot pursuit.

By the time the cousins reached the large field of *ichu*, they were out of breath. Even so, they set to work collecting bunches of grass and egg-sized stones. As K'uchi-Wara put it, "This is our *real* work." They quickly wove the grass into vaguely human figures several feet high, which they lined up against a rock outcrop. Every so often, they glanced toward the slowly moving herd.

"*You* can take the first shot," said K'uchi-Wara.

"Thanks, that's *big* of you."

Neither boy went anywhere without his sling, which he kept in a cloth bag. Opening the bag that hung at his waist, Jukumari pulled out a long stout cord made from spun and braided llama wool. In the middle of the cord was a shallow pouch or cradle to hold the stone. He fitted a stone to this cradle. Holding both ends of the cord in his right hand, he began to swing the sling in a wide arc over his head. Faster and faster it went. When he let go of one end, the snapping of the cord produced a CRACK. It sent the projectile hurtling toward a grass figure ... narrowly missing it. The stone struck the outcrop behind the figure and ricocheted.

Oh, Jukumari, you're such an oaf. But that's what I love about you. You've never been able to outshoot me, yet you don't give up hope. I've been practicing with slings since Uncle gave me the little cord six years ago. I've gotten so good that I can outshoot all the other boys in Wila-Nayra. And many of the men too! Maybe one day you'll beat me. Until then ... K'uchi-Wara confidently stepped in front of his cousin. *This is so much fun!* His sling, which had been braided by his father, was mostly white in color, but with alternating bands of black and white at either end. He stuck a rounded stone in the pouch and started swinging the cord. His eyes were fixed on the target. When the missile had gained enough momentum, he released it. CRACK. The stone went speeding toward one of the grass figures ... whizzzzz ... smashing it to pieces.

So went the morning. As the sun moved directly overhead, the cousins shared a meager meal of roasted potato. Afterwards they hurried to catch up with the alpacas. Their charges had been drifting steadily along.

* * *

Back at the homestead, K'uchi-Wara's father decided it was time to plant the "early" potatoes, so he went rummaging around in an old storage shed. The extended family kept many useful items there. There were different types of rope, weapons such as slings and clubs, and various farming implements. He finally found what he was looking for: a footplow and a clodcrusher. He checked the footplow to make sure it was still in good shape. The leather thongs binding the wooden handle and footrest to the stout digging stick—the point of which had been hardened by sticking it in a fire, though not long enough to burn it—were still taut. Then he examined the clodcrusher. He noticed that the leather strips used to haft the river cobble to the lengthy handle had come loose, and spent several moments tightening them. Then he carried the tools to the family's potato garden, going through a break in the oval wall.

K'uchi-Wara's parents spent the afternoon working in the garden. Although his father was the leader of Wila-Nayra, he had to do manual labor, just like everyone else. While he employed the footplow to break up the compact soil and turn it over, the mother used the clodcrusher to do exactly what the tool's name implies. Next they spread fertilizer— pulverized llama and alpaca dung—evenly over the field. The task completed, the father stood up and wiped the sweat from his brow. "Let's take a break," he suggested. From the woven bag that hung from his shoulder he produced some coca leaves. He shared them with his wife. They spent a brief period sitting together, side by side, each with lump in cheek, neither speaking. Both were content to be in the other's company. When their coca break ended, they returned to work with renewed energy. K'uchi-Wara's father started digging small holes, one every foot or so, across the surface of the garden. The mother followed, carrying a bag of seed potatoes. She dropped two or three into each hole, and filled it with earth.

* * *

It was early evening. The boys sat on a rocky incline. From their vantage point, they had a good view of the mountain meadow below them, where the alpacas fed placidly and hummed. The shadows were lengthening as the sun drifted lazily toward the horizon. The peaks around them were coming into sharp focus, and a general tranquility was settling over the land. K'uchi-Wara was facing his cousin. He was about to say something, when out of the corner of his eye he caught a hint of movement among some boulders. Looking to his right, he saw a flash of white. Then it was gone. "D-did you see that?"

"See what?" Jukumari could tell from the slight tremor in his cousin's voice that he was serious.

"I thought I saw something. Something moving back there."

They both turned and scanned the boulders. Nothing. They listened intently. Nothing. K'uchi-Wara began to realize it was *too* quiet. *Where's the chirping of the little birds that fly around the mountain slopes? Where are the sounds made by the vizcachas as they scamper over rocks? What's hap-*

pened to the humming of the flock? All had become deathly silent. K'uchi-Wara turned back toward the incline and gazed down at the alpacas. They seemed agitated, with their heads held high, their ears pricked up. They were looking around with jerky movements.

"This place is making me real nervous!" said Jukumari. "Let's get out of here!"

They gathered their things, especially their slings, and ran full speed down the hill to the pasture. They roused the animals with a "*ch'uy, ch'uy,*" setting them on the path toward home.

As soon as he reached his house, K'uchi-Wara breathlessly recounted his experience to his parents. "What do you think I saw up there?"

His father became thoughtful. "I'm not sure. But it could've been a *supaya.* I've heard it said that the *supaya* sometimes takes human form. And it's been known to dress in white."

"But what is it?" the child asked.

"Your grandfather told me, and he knew a lot about such things, it's an unhappy soul. When a person dies, his spirit makes the long journey back to its home at the heart of the mountain. If it loses its way, it may become trapped in our world. Then it becomes a *supaya.*"

"What does it do? Can it hurt you?"

"It mostly lives in the ground and eats dirt. But it may come to resent the living. As its resentment builds, it may start playing nasty tricks on us. If it's especially miserable, it may even try to kill people. It can knock rocks onto its victims and crush them. Or it can infect them with illness. So yes, it can be *very* dangerous! If you come across one again, I want you to get away from it."

"Don't worry," said the boy, "if I meet a *supaya* face-to-face, I'll turn and *run* as fast as I can!"

K'uchi-Wara helps his uncle slaughter and butcher an alpaca

Chapter Five: A Break From Herding

Most days, K'uchi-Wara and Jukumari followed the same routine. They took a group of llamas and alpacas to a high meadow, watched the animals graze, and practiced with their slings. Sometimes, though, they got a break from this routine.

The sky was clear, the sun bright. Its warmth took the bite out of the morning air. K'uchi-Wara's father had called together his three brothers, their six sons, and his own child, all of whom were seated on the patio. They waited patiently for him to speak. K'uchi-Wara sat by Jukumari.

"Today," the father began, addressing the boys, "we're going to teach you how to slaughter and butcher livestock. We're going to show you the right way to do these tasks. The first step is to decide which animals to slaughter. Let's go to the small corral."

K'uchi-Wara and the others crossed the yard to a circular wall. It was made from irregular stones set in a mortar of adobe, and measured ten paces across. Pulling himself up the wall so that his chin was even with the top, the boy peered over. What he saw broke his heart. Inside were a dozen of the scruffiest and most pathetic looking creatures imaginable. Among them was a frail female alpaca with long black wool.

"Oh, no!" K'uchi-Wara wailed. "We're going to kill Killima-Awicha (the 'charcoal-colored grandmother')? She's been around forever."

"She's twice your age, son. That's the problem. She's so old, she's lost her teeth. She can't chew *ichu* anymore, and is beginning to starve.

To be kind, we have to put her out of her misery. She's led a good life, though, and has produced lots of young."

As the group entered the dung-filled corral, K'uchi-Wara's father explained why they would be slaughtering the other animals. "Take this gelding here," he said, calling attention to a large llama with a dark brown coat, white face, and white stockings. "It's too weak to carry loads." K'uchi-Wara could see that the beast was feeble. When he ran his hand over its rump, he could feel the bones sticking up beneath the skin. His father pointed out several females: one with light brown fleece, another with reddish-brown wool and a black face, a third with a pied coat of white, black, and brown. "They can no longer bear young."

K'uchi-Wara led a brown llama with black stockings from the corral. As the animal was crippled, it walked with difficulty. He guided it to a flat area at the edge of the homestead that had been cleared of vegetation. The three sacred mountains, with Qala-Uta in the middle, appeared to loom over the event.

His father declared, "Here's the right way to slay a llama." He pushed the old animal to the ground and tied its legs together with rope. "I don't want to be kicked." He took a bronze knife and drew it across the neck, opening a gaping wound. The bright blood came in spurts. They coincided with the beast's heartbeats. The flow was strong at first, but quickly ebbed. The llama's muscles became taut as it tried to struggle, then went limp. "Now," the father continued, "we gut it." He untied the legs and rolled the animal onto its back. He made an incision down the middle of its body from the neck to the pelvis and across the belly. Opening the chest cavity, he pulled out the organs. They were wet and shiny. They varied in color from a delicate pink to a rich purple. He cleaned the cavity as best he could, and showed the boys how to skin the llama. He worked quickly and skillfully. All the while, he explained what he was doing and why. "After we tan the tough hide, we'll use it to make rope and moccasins and other useful things. But the tanning will have to wait for another time."

K'uchi-Wara's father cut chunks of fat from the carcass and tossed them into a large bowl. When he was done, his told his son, "Take this to your mother so she can render the fat and make tallow." Then he carved slabs of meat from the bones. Meanwhile his youngest brother, Jukumari's father, cut the slabs into long thin strips that he hung from a wooden rack. They would freeze-dry in the air to produce *ch'arkhi.* By the end of the butchering process, nothing was left of the llama but a skeleton. Whereas a few bones would be boiled to make broth, most were buried so they did not attract scavengers.

During the days that followed, K'uchi-Wara and his cousins helped their fathers to slaughter and butcher the remaining animals in the corral. It was a difficult and messy business.

A month later, as measured by the changing phases of the moon, the boy got another break from his routine. Over breakfast, his father told him that they would be taking a trip.

"Where are we going?" said the child with great interest.

"Downslope to another village."

"How come?"

"Some of our kin are gathering there. I thought it about time that you met them. They'll be coming from communities near and far. We'll be taking most of the goods from our butchering sessions, including the hides, *ch'arkhi,* and tallow. So I want you to get three llamas ready."

A short time later, K'uchi-Wara and his father were heading down the rocky trail, driving the heavily laden llamas before them. The day was overcast and blustery. K'uchi-Wara drew his mantle tightly about his shoulders. The farther down-slope they went, the broader, gentler, and greener the mountain became. The sun, a pale orb partly obscured by clouds, was almost overhead when they arrived at the top of a little knob and looked down on the village. It consisted of a collection of houses that were more tightly bunched than those of Wila-Nayra.

"That's where we're headed," the father said. "I want you to remember the details of this trip. What goes on here is important for our family."

K'uchi-Wara stood on the patio of a stone house much like his own and met his more distant relatives. He never realized that he had so many. One man, who was from a community located in a valley to the west, clapped him on the back. He said, "K'uchi-Wara, I haven't seen you since ... let me see ... since your First Haircutting. You were only knee high then. This is the first time you've come to our gathering, isn't it?"

The boy nodded.

"And what have you brought us?"

"Well, sir, we have hides and tallow and *ch'arkhi*. Last month, my cousins and I learned how to slaughter llamas and alpacas. My dad also showed us how to cut them up."

"Very good. You know, your family makes the best llama-jerky on the mountain. I have some dried corn, fresh greens, and pottery to exchange with you. How does that sound?"

"Good, I suppose. But how come you have to trade with us? Why don't you produce your own hides and fat and dried meat?"

"The valley where I live is too low for raising llamas and alpacas. They like it where it's higher and cooler. So we have to rely on you to supply us with those animal products."

"I see! And we live too high to grow corn and greens. Also there's no clay around Wila-Nayra for making pottery."

"Smart boy."

If K'uchi-Wara was surprised to see a cousin from a distant valley, he was delighted to meet a relative from an even more exotic place. "Are you *really* from the *yunka*? You're not kidding, are you?"

"Yes and no."

"Huh?"

"Yes, I'm *really* from the *yunka*," said the man, laughing. "And no, I'm not kidding."

"What's the *yunka* like?"

"It's very different from where you live. For one thing, it's *green* on the eastern slope of the Andes. The vegetation's so thick, you have to fight to get through it. And you often get heavy mists that hang low over the valleys, drenching everything. It's beautiful."

"Have you ever seen a monkey? Or a parrot? Or an anteater?" One of K'uchi-Wara's uncles had told him tall tales about such creatures. He was skeptical of their existence, though.

"Of course. Many times."

"R-e-a-l-l-y?" the child said, his eyes wide. "Can I visit you? I never get to go anywhere! This village is the farthest I've ever been from home. What did you bring us from the *yunka*? A jaguar?"

"I'm afraid not," the man laughed again. "I've got more useful things. Like coca and dried chili peppers and salt."

"Oh." K'uchi-Wara could not hide his disappointment.

Before the boy and his father left for home, they packed all the goods they had gotten and loaded them onto the backs of the llamas. They said their goodbyes and set off. When they reached their homestead, they would divide the goods equally between the four families.

Several large festivals were held in Wila-Nayra during the year. K'uchi-Wara's favorite, which took place in February at the height of the rainy season, honored their livestock. It was at the start of this celebration that the boy woke early and left the house. He carefully closed the door behind him. Despite it being summer, the morning was chilly. He knew from experience, though, that as soon as the sun appeared from behind the ridge to the east, its rays would warm the land.

Walking to a square corral, he entered. With loud shouts he roused its occupants, and singled out six alpacas. They were his personal animals. He could easily recognize them based on the color and texture of their wool, on the patterning of their coats, and on the color of their eyes.

K'uchi-Wara went up to one of the females he had received for his First Haircutting. Gazing into a blue eye, he said, "You're my pride and joy." He ran his fingers through her fine white wool. Then he glanced at the newborn beside her and smiled. It looked just like her.

He led his six alpacas from the corral. At his request, his father had pierced their ears with a bone awl. Now he attached a large tassel of red and yellow yarn to the top of each triangular ear. "You look ever so festive," he told them. Next he rubbed red earth on their coats to give them health and make them fertile. Near the homestead were thick clumps of vegetation, which at this time of year were covered with flowers. He picked as many yellow, white and purple blossoms as he could and wove them into garlands. As he worked, he sang a little song that his mother had taught him:

> Oh, mighty condor,
> Owner of the skies,
> Take me back home,
> Up to the lofty spires.
>
> Oh, mighty condor,
> Let's fly to my land,
> To see my brothers,
> And lend them a hand!

When he finished making the garlands, he placed them around the necks of his animals. Unfortunately one of the alpacas was able to curl its long lips around the garland. K'uchi-Wara shouted, "Stop that!" But the flowers disappeared.

After breakfast, the child's father blessed the extended family's llamas and alpacas by sprinkling them with beer made from fermented *quinua*. The family subsequently picked the animals that would represent their herd in the community-wide festival. K'uchi-Wara was proud that his female—decorated with the ear-tassels, red earth, and garland—was among the chosen.

As the sun neared the top of its climb, the inhabitants of Wila-Nayra gathered at a flat bare space in the middle of the gentle slope. This was their plaza. They arrived with their prized llamas and alpacas. Before long, the plaza had become a shifting mass of a hundred people and twice that many animals. K'uchi-Wara's father, as headman, honored the assembled livestock by flecking them with *quinua-chicha*. By extension, he blessed all the llamas and alpacas that belonged to the community. Then he made an offering to Qala-Uta and the other two peaks by spitting beer in their direction.

Addressing Qala-Uta, he prayed in Aymara: "*Nanakan awquisa*, 'our father,' we thank you with all our hearts for sending rain. It sustains the *ichu* grass that nourishes our alpacas. We thank you with all our hearts for making our animals fertile. You have bestowed many young on us. We thank you with all our hearts for protecting our livestock. You shield them from storm, hail, and lightning."

When the shadows started to lengthen, K'uchi-Wara and his relatives walked up-slope from their homestead to a family shrine. It was hidden among some boulders. It looked like a tiny stone house. While the group arranged themselves in a semicircle around the front, K'uchi-Wara knelt and reached into it. Suddenly he jerked his hand away. Jumping up and back, he let out a SQUAWK. A big black spider crawled from within and scurried to the rocks, where it disappeared. His kin roared with laughter. Red faced, the child tentatively stuck his hand back in and withdrew a stone that looked vaguely like a llama. Doing so, his father blessed it, doused it with *chicha*, and said, "Little *illa*, make our llamas and alpacas fertile." K'uchi-Wara pulled out six more *illas*, one after another, while his father repeated the rite. The family built a small bonfire into which they tossed llama fat, coca leaves, chili peppers, flowers, a dried llama fetus, and other offerings.

The festival continued the next day. The highlight was to be a race between boys from different families. It would start at the plaza, continue up the steep slope, and finish at the pools. While the route may have been straightforward, the event had a twist: each boy had to drive before him a llama buck. The victor would not be the person, but rather the animal that reached the mountain's "eyes" first. Although the race was supposed to be fun and entertaining, it had a serious side. As K'uchi-Wara's father explained to his people, "It is meant to honor Qala-Uta. The winning llama will be held in high esteem by the mountain-deity, and the champion boy will have good luck throughout the year."

K'uchi-Wara begged his father to let him compete. His father agreed. So in the morning the child went to a square corral and chose as his running-mate the largest male in the herd. The animal had a light brown coat with big white patches. To make sure everyone knew that it was *his* llama, the boy decorated its banana-shaped ears with brightly colored tassels. He smeared red earth on its sides, and hung a flower-wreath around its neck.

The race took place at midday. A dozen boys, including K'uchi-Wara, formed a line across the plaza. In front of them was another line made up of a dozen bucks. Flanking the lines on either side was a mob of excited spectators. "K'UCHI-WARA, K'UCHI-WARA!" chanted one noisy group. In his hand the boy held his sling, which he would use to control the llama.

"Are the contestants ready?" barked the village headman. "Then RUN!"

K'uchi-Wara lunged forward shouting, "CH'UY, CH'UY, CH'UY!" He cracked his sling like a whip. His llama bolted toward the mountain-slope. Some of the boys, though, were either less skilled with their slings or less lucky because their bucks became confused. They charged into the crowd, causing chaos and panic.

When K'uchi-Wara's llama reached the foot of the rocky slope, it began to slow. He cracked his sling again, sending the animal scrambling upward. He ran after it. He glanced around. Three other boys were even with him, which made him run faster. Up and up he went. He was sweating heavily now. Due to the dryness of the air, however, the sweat quickly evaporated. He noticed that his buck was going too far to the left, so he flicked his sling, catching the animal on its left flank and sending it more to the right. "CH'UY, CH'UY!" he yelled. He looked to either side again. He had left the competition behind. *Good thing because I'm tired. I think my heart's going to explode.* The slope was beginning to ease. He did not have far to go. *I can do this! I can do this!*

Then he took a misstep. As his leg slipped out from under him, he slammed into the ground. Hard! A sharp pain shot through his knee. He heard a collective groan from far below. Floating on the breeze, it had come from a particular group of spectators in the plaza. He stood. He felt woozy. He had the metallic taste of blood in his mouth, having bitten his tongue when he fell. Another boy was catching up to him. The guy was passing him! He turned back toward the slope and started hobbling upward. He took his sling and cracked it, sending his buck toward the prize. *Where's that other kid's llama? Has it already reached the "eyes"?* Distant cheers erupted from the crowd in the plaza. *I've lost.* He stopped running. He stood, head bowed, panting. He looked up and past the figure of his competitor, who was still heading toward the finish line. *Wait. What's that standing at a pool and lapping water?*

A feast was held that evening. K'uchi-Wara was gnawing on a llama rib, trying to get the last bits of meat from it, when a girl approached. She was a little shorter than him, and skinny. She had a pretty face, with large dark eyes and jet-black hair that fell straight down her back. She looked to be about his age. Other than close relatives, he had had little contact with members of the opposite sex. He was intrigued.

"Hi," she said, "I'm Nina ('fire'). My parents call me that because they say I have a strong personality. What's your name?"

"K'uchi-Wara."

"That's a nice name. A bit unusual, though. You know, I was watching from the plaza when you won the big race."

"You mean you watched my *buck* win!"

"You're being modest. Your llama finished first because after you fell you were able to get back on your feet and urge it onward. Otherwise the other kid's buck would've won."

"I guess so."

"You *guess* so? You don't sound very excited. It's a great honor to be first. Now you're Qala-Uta's favorite! Come walk with me."

K'uchi-Wara dropped the bone he was holding. He wiped his greasy hands on his tunic, and pushed himself up off the ground. Then he and Nina strolled away from the plaza. They went to a more secluded spot where they were hidden from view by a little knoll. Nobody minded. They took a seat.

"You know," said the girl, eyeing K'uchi-Wara, "you're kind of cute."

"You're not so bad yourself."

"Thanks. Uhh, there's something I've been wondering ..."

"Yeah? What's that?"

"Well ...," she continued, "I've been told that boys are different from girls. And I want to know, is it true?"

"I've heard the same thing. But I'm not sure if it's true because ... uh ... to be honest ... uh ... I've never *seen* a girl."

"Hmm. Tell you what, K'uchi-Wara. Why don't we play a little game. If you'll show me yours, I'll show you mine."

"Okay, but you go first."

"Sure." Nina wore a typical Lupaka dress that extended from her shoulders to her ankles. It was held in place by a belt. Carefully removing the belt from around her waist, she opened her dress so K'uchi-Wara could take a look.

"How odd! Are all girls like that?"

"I think so. Now it's your turn."

He lifted his tunic for Nina to see.

She scrutinized him for a long time. Then she asked, "How come yours goes out, while mine goes in?"

"I don't know."

So went the evening. The next day, K'uchi-Wara went back to his normal routine of herding, a bit wiser about the world.

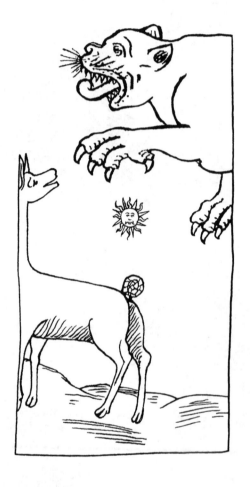

The snow-white puma attacks one of K'uchi-Wara's alpacas

Chapter Six: The Puma

As a person ages, he can get stuck in a rut. If he follows the same routine over and over, rejecting variety and spontaneity, his life will become rigidly patterned. Then all his days will seem the same. They will start to blur into one another, and time will appear to speed up. His days will trickle into months, the months will flow by and become years, the years will gush into decades, and the decades will surge into the future. In the end, the elder will look back over his life and wonder: *Where did the time go?*

The same cannot be said of a child. Each day brings with it the promise of something new: a novel experience, a fresh possibility, an unexpected adventure. Although K'uchi-Wara spent much of his time shepherding llamas and alpacas, he faced each sunrise with wide-eyed wonder.

* * *

It was May, the start of the dry season. K'uchi-Wara was eating break-fast on the patio with his parents. His father said to him, "Your cousins have come down with a strange illness. They're all confined to their sleeping-platforms. That includes Jukumari. But the animals still need to be grazed ..."

"So you want me to take a herd out by myself?" the boy interrupted.

"Yes. Though I don't think it's good for children to shepherd alone."

"Why not?"

"Two reasons. First, there's the question of safety. What would you do if you were on the mountain with your alpacas and you twisted an ankle? There'd be no one to help you."

"I could limp home."

"You miss the point. The second reason to work with another person is that it teaches the importance of complementary pairs."

Oh, no! thought K'uchi-Wara. *He's going to give me another lecture. Why is it that every time I talk to my parents, they try to teach me something?*

The man saw his child roll his eyes. He said, "This is important! As I've explained many times, the idea of complementary pairs is basic to our beliefs. It's part of what makes us Lupaka. And it's something you need to understand if you're going to take over as headman. The idea is that each thing in the world has an opposite that must be paired with it in order to complete it. Without its opposite, it's useless. So you have me and your mother, as male and female ..."

I know all about that, thanks to Nina.

"... me and the other villagers, as headman and commoners; the mummies and us, as ancestors and descendants.

"I'm getting off the subject, though. What I'm trying to say is that I don't like it when you work alone. And I know that I'm giving you a lot of responsibility. But you'll be on your own today."

K'uchi-Wara was thrilled. Even so, he said, "How come you can't help me, Dad?"

"I have to go down to the next village. I need to pick up a bag of corn."

"How about *you*, Mom? How come you can't come with me?"

"I'm going to be busy weaving. Now that your father's fixed my loom, I can finish the tunic I'm making for you. Don't worry, though. You'll be *fine!*"

The couple sent their son to rouse forty alpacas in a rectangular corral. As he was leaving, he heard his mother say, "Are you sure he'll be okay? He's only eight."

His father replied, "He's a smart kid. He can handle it. Besides, we don't want to spoil him. But if it makes you feel better, I'll try to return before dark and go help him."

K'uchi-Wara took his charges up the slope to the pools, where he let them drink. Then he led them to a pasture. He found a comfortable spot on an incline overlooking the grazing land, sat, and looked out over his family's animals. *We're lucky that so many of our females have babies.* They had given birth in December and January. That was when the bunchgrasses were most plentiful, and they could produce the most milk. *I have to be careful, though. The young animals are still small, so they'd make easy prey. Until they're weaned, I have to protect them as best I can.* Among the mothers he was tending was the female with blue eyes and white wool.

Without Jukumari's company, K'uchi-Wara grew bored. After gazing at his beloved alpacas, he practiced with his sling. But his favorite pastime was far less fun when there was nobody to compete against, even though out-shooting his cousin wasn't much of a challenge. He ate a roasted potato for lunch. In the late afternoon, he watched the wind moving in waves through the green grass, the puffy clouds drifting across a blue sky. He became so sluggish that he fell asleep.

The boy woke. Raising his arms above his head, he stretched. The shadows around him were lengthening. In the golden light of evening, the surrounding peaks stood out starkly, their great bulk accentuated. They seemed to be crowding one another. It was as if they were jockeying for a better view of the child and what was about to happen. He became aware of a strange silence. He stood and surveyed the herd in the meadow below. The animals were on edge. Their heads were erect, their ears cocked. *Why are they so nervous?* As this thought was going through his mind, he realized that he too felt uneasy. To the boy's right was a low ridge of broken rock, which marked the edge of the pasture. Jutting out of the mountain slope around the ridge were outcrops of bedrock.

K'uchi-Wara caught a flash of white behind a rock. A second later, he saw movement behind the ridge. *Something's lurking along the backside of those rocks. Something's trying to reach the meadow unseen. Something's after my alpacas!* The child crept down the incline to the pasture. He kept an eye on the ridge of broken rock. When he reached the first tufts of bunchgrass, he pulled his sling from the woven bag he carried. He bent down to pick up a stone, his gaze unwavering. Inching toward the herd of agitated alpacas, he fitted the stone to the sling's pouch and held both ends of the cord in his left hand. Still moving forward, he began to swing the sling.

A white mass exploded outward. It shot toward his favorite alpaca's offspring. K'uchi-Wara was so startled that he nearly dropped his sling. The puma was as long as a man is tall, and outweighed an adult alpaca. It was solid muscle. The most extraordinary thing about the beast, however, was its coat. From the top of its head to the tip of its tail it was the color of new-fallen snow. Before the boy grasped what was going on, the puma pounced on the young alpaca, knocking it to the ground. The mother, in a blind panic, let out some ear-piercing bleats and kicked at the cat with its powerful hind-legs. The puma paid the mother little attention as it grabbed for the baby's throat.

Just then everything came into sharp focus for K'uchi-Wara: he saw the white beast standing over its hapless prey, he saw the hysterical mother, and he saw himself with his sling. It was as if he were a detached observer looking down from above. He watched as he swung the woven cord in a broad arc. Faster and faster it went. CRACK. He sent the stone flying toward the cat ... but grazed its scalp. The puma's head shot up. It was furious that it should be disturbed before it had had a chance to feed. It looked right at the boy with golden eyes. It let out a low gravelly growl, which rose in pitch and volume until it culminated in a blood-curdling scream. It started towards him, slowly at first, then picking up speed. It intended to kill him. The child reached down for a rock, his hand trembling. Closer the animal came. He stuck the rock in the sling. Closer the animal came. He swung the cord around his head, his eyes never leaving the target. Still closer the cat came. As it leapt—its claws extended, its mouth wide, its fangs bared—he released the projectile. The two loud CRACKs were almost simultaneous. The cat hit the boy, knocking him to the ground. Scarlet blood trickled from a fracture in the animal's skull, staining its snow-white coat. A golden eye rolled around in its massive head. Then the beast died. K'uchi-Wara shoved it off of him and started shaking uncontrollably. Possibly it was out of relief, perhaps it was due to a need to release his pent-up emotions, or maybe it was because he was only eight. He sat down and cried and cried.

* * *

As the sun, a great fireball, sank below the horizon, the child's father walked up the path to the meadow. He was looking for his son. He had gone to the next community and returned to Wila-Nayra with the corn. Now he wanted to get the herd back to their homestead before it was completely dark. As he came up over a rise, he saw the boy, small and vulnerable, seated on the ground. The boy was holding his head in his hands. *What's going on? What's that lying next to my child? It looks like ... like ...*

K'uchi-Wara's father dresses in his finest clothing and adornments

Chapter Seven: The Apu-Panaka

K'uchi-Wara's fame spread quickly. The inhabitants of Wila-Nayra and the other villages on the mountain talked nonstop about how he had killed the *khunu-titi* or "snow-cat." Pilgrims arrived at his homestead, wanting to meet him. They asked to see the pelt of the great puma too. K'uchi-Wara's mother had spent a good deal of time and effort to preserve it. She had skinned the creature, stretched its hide over a wooden frame, scraped the flesh from it, and smoked it. People debated whether the child and pelt were *waqas*. Anything unusual could be a *waqa*, which was thought to have sacred power. The consensus was that a giant snow-colored puma qualified. So did a boy who was not only brave enough, but skilled enough with his sling, to kill such a beast.

There was endless speculation on the exact nature of the *khunu-titi*. Everyone agreed that it was not a *supaya*. Then what? Perhaps it was the cat of a powerful mountain-god such as Qala-Uta. Some people went further, claiming it was a *qoa*, an ill-tempered spirit with a cat-like form. The *qoa* was greatly feared. When it got angry it was said to fly through the air, shooting hail from its eyes and ears, and lightning bolts from its rear. The hail was dangerous because it could flatten crops. Lightning could wipe out the Lupaka and their alpacas. So these spirits had to be kept happy with regular offerings of guinea pigs, beer, and llama fat. The more knowledgeable folks taking part in the discussions, though, pointed out that it could not be a *qoa* because such creatures were supernatural and could not be killed.

There was long and heated debate over the consequences of the puma's death. A vocal few, mostly people living in more distant villages who did not know the boy, said he had been wicked to slay the creature. But they ignored the fact that he had acted in self-defense. They fretted that Qala-Uta, to whom the cat may have belonged, might blame everyone in the region for its death and punish them. Such a powerful mountain-god could destroy them with cold, wind, snow, storms, or floods. Most folks, however, especially the residents of Wila-Nayra, took a more reasonable view. They felt that if Qala-Uta had not wanted the child to kill his cat, he would have stopped it from happening. They also said that since he had allowed it—as well as had empowered the boy to win the llama race during the February festival—he must love K'uchi-Wara. The child should be held in high esteem!

* * *

Shortly after the puma was slain, the residents of Wila-Nayra received word that they would be visited by an Apu-Panaka. Given that K'uchi-Wara's father was the community headman, the Apu-Panaka would certainly want to meet him.

On the day of the visit, the child woke and breakfasted with his parents. "This is so exciting!" he told them. "I've never seen an Apu-Panaka, or any Inka official. I wonder what he'll be like. And why is he coming here?"

Good question, his father thought. *What do the Inkas want with us?*

The father dressed in an elegant outfit befitting his position as headman. He only wore it for special events. He put on a beautiful tunic decorated with vertical stripes of burgundy, green, and beige that his wife had spent months weaving. He also donned his silver bracelet, black headband, double-crescent pendant, and llama-hide moccasins. Lastly he wrapped his mantle about his shoulders.

The mother called K'uchi-Wara to her. "Here," she said, handing him a brand-new tunic. "I've been waiting for a special occasion to give it to you. This seems like a good time. I finished making it last month. I hope you like it."

The boy took the garment and held it up, pretending to inspect it with a critical eye. It was all black. His mother had decorated it, though, by sewing a red fringe to the bottom hem. Adopting a blasé attitude, he said, "Well ... I guess it will *have* to do." But then, seeing the dejected look on his mother's face, he changed his tone. "You know that I'm kidding, Mom. It's great! Can I wear it for the Apu-Panaka's visit?"

"Why do you think I'm giving it to you *now*. Go change."

The royal official, together with his entourage, approached the homestead in the early afternoon. K'uchi-Wara and his parents were waiting on the patio. When the child caught sight of him, he tugged at his father's arm and said, "Look how colorful his tunic is."

The man was dressed in a knee-length sleeveless tunic of alpaca wool, whose front was decorated with a special pattern. Whereas most of the piece was royal blue, a large yellow square covered the lower third of it. Within the large square were four smaller ones of blue. And at the center of each blue square was a tiny red one.

As the Apu-Panaka got closer, K'uchi-Wara whispered to his father, "Have you ever seen such riches? He makes *you* look like a beggar, Dad." On his wrist the official wore a gold bracelet, in his ears were large silver ear-spools, and circling his head with its closely-cropped hair was a green band. Attached to the front of the band was a silver plaque shaped like an hourglass.

Reaching the house, the Apu-Panaka greeted them. As a gesture of friendship, he withdrew several coca leaves from the cloth bag he carried. He offered them to K'uchi-Wara's father, who reciprocated. They chewed coca before getting down to business.

"I've come to meet your son." the official announced. He spoke Quechua, the state's common tongue. The child and his parents could understand and talk to him as they had been required to learn the language; the Inkas had commanded that the members of the nobility, even people living in the provinces, know Quechua. "Since your boy killed the snow-cat, he's become known throughout the region. Some people even say he's a *waqa*. Is that him?" he asked, pointing at the child.

"Yes," the father replied. "K'uchi-Wara, come over here."

As the boy stood before him, the official said, "Is it true you single-handedly slew the snow-beast with your sling?"

"Yes . . . gulp . . . sir."

"Speak up, child! What's that you say?"

"Yes, sir."

"You certainly are brave. And you're decidedly the darling of the local mountain-god! I'd like to invite you to Cuzco to take part in the *qhapaq hucha* celebrations. Would you like that?"

A numbness came over K'uchi-Wara's father as the Apu-Panaka's words hit home. *I have to remain calm,* he told himself, taking several deep breaths.

"I guess so," answered the boy.

"You *guess* so? Don't you know that this is a once-in-a-lifetime opportunity? Just think, you'll tour our beautiful capital, participate in the festival with other children, and if you're lucky, see the king. Wayna Qhapaq's a living god, you know. Doesn't that sound exciting?"

"Yes, sir."

The father was watching his wife when she realized the implications of what the dignitary was saying. Her eyes grew wide. "I'm sorry"—her breath caught in her throat—"but my Quechua isn't very good. Aren't the *qhapaq huchas* ..."

"Sacrificial victims."

"So you want to take my son ... for sa — sa ... as an offering?"

"Well, yes."

The blood drained from the woman's face. For a moment, her husband thought she was going to collapse. He put his arm out to steady her. Regaining her composure somewhat, she waved him away and said, "But I thought the *qhapaq huchas* had to be flawless children. That they couldn't have any blemishes!"

"That's very true."

"Then my son would never do! Look, he has warts. K'uchi-Wara, show the man your hands. And he has a scar on his chin. He fell as a toddler. So he'd never be acceptable to the gods! If you were to offer him, they'd be angry. They'd punish you!"

"Dear lady, we've already established that your boy is loved by Qala-Uta. The mountain-god hasn't rejected him because of some ... um ... minor flaws. In fact, I believe he's specifically chosen the child to serve him!"

"But ... but ..."

"Think of the benefits," the Apu-Panaka interrupted her, "of having a son who's a *qhapaq hucha*! Your husband will become the ruler of the whole region, of all its communities and inhabitants. Since *voluntarily* placing a child in the service of a god is such a noble act, you'll both gain prestige. You'll be forever honored. As for the boy, he'll become like the condor, an intermediary between Qala-Uta and your people. If there's a drought and your potato plants begin to wither, he'll be in a position to help by getting the mountain-deity to send rain. Should your alpacas be plagued by disease or become infertile, you'll be able to pray to him. He'll have the power to step in and make your animals strong again. And he'll be able to protect your people from cold, hail, and lightning! We've discussed the matter enough for today, though. I'll leave and give you a chance to consider what I've said. I'll return tomorrow to see what you've decided about your son's future." The official departed, followed by his entourage.

The parents sent K'uchi-Wara out to play. Meanwhile they shut themselves in the house and discussed what to do. The mother spoke, switching from Quechua to Aymara, "By all the gods in the sky, this can't be happening. It just *can't* be happening!"

"Yeah," her husband responded, "I keep thinking that I'm in the middle of a horrible dream. And keep hoping that I'll wake and everything'll be okay."

"There must be some mistake. That's all there is to it. Why would the Inkas want to punish us? And to punish K'uchi-Wara? He's only a child. I'm getting the shivers just thinking about what they want to do to him. Hand me my mantle, will you?"

"Sure," her husband said as he pulled her garment from a peg on the wall and wrapped it around here shoulders. He held her tightly in his arms. "I don't think K'uchi-Wara really understands what it means to be a *qhapaq hucha*."

"No, he doesn't. Damn! Damn! Damn! This is so unfair!"

"I know! Did we do something wrong to deserve this? Could we have done things differently and avoided it? If I hadn't sent the boy off to herd alone, he'd never have killed the snow-cat. Then he wouldn't have come to the Inkas' attention."

"Well, if I hadn't spent the day weaving, and had gone with him, we wouldn't be in this terrible mess."

"Wait, we can't blame ourselves for what's happened. It's the Inkas who are responsible. Not us!"

"The Apu-Panaka's the one to blame." She freed herself from her husband's embrace. Then, clenching her fists so hard that the knuckles turned white, she said through gritted teeth, "The bastard! Can you believe his arrogance? He actually thinks we'll hand K'uchi-Wara over to him. Voluntarily, no less!"

"Yeah, but the question is, what can we do to avoid it?"

"Well, when the Apu-Panaka returns, we'll simply tell him that he *can't* have the child!"

"I don't think that'll work. His men will just seize the boy by force."

"Okay, we'll try to reason with him. We'll have a talk. We'll convince him that K'uchi-Wara's *not* the best choice to be a *qhapaq hucha*."

"You already tried that approach; the Apu-Panaka wasn't persuaded by your argument that the child's blemished."

"Well, we could tell him the boy isn't a virgin! That he had sex with Nina, and so is unfit to serve Qala-Uta."

"The Apu-Panaka would never believe it. He knows full well that the child's body isn't fully developed, and that he's not yet capable of having sex. Why do you think the Inkas choose boys under the age of ten to be victims? It's so they don't have to worry about the children being virgins."

"Then we'll have to come up with another reason for why the Inkas can't have him."

"What other reasons could we possibly give the man to get him to change his mind? The fact is the boy *did* kill a monstrous puma. The only way I know to explain the miracle is to accept that Qala-Uta protected him. And guided his arm as he used his sling, which means that the mountain-god truly loves him. So maybe Qala-Uta really *does* want the child to serve him."

"Whose side are you on, anyway?"

"You know that I want what's best for K'uchi-Wara, the same as you! It's just that I don't see any way of convincing the Apu-Panaka *not* to take the child. He seems dead set on it."

"How about if we bribe him?"

"Bribe him? What are we supposed to offer him? He already has wealth. You saw his adornments. And his clothing all but *trumpets* his status and power. The best we could give him would be a sack-full of potatoes!"

"Don't — mock — me!"

"I'm not. I'm just being realistic. And I'm telling you—there's nothing we own that could possibly tempt the man."

The woman continued, "Then we have to hide the boy. We'll send him to live with relatives in a distant village. Maybe in the *yunka*. The Inkas'll never find him there!"

The husband sighed. "You're grasping at straws! They'd return here, seize us, and torture us. How long do you think we could hold out before we revealed K'uchi-Wara's whereabouts? They'd also punish our kin and the rest of Wila-Nayra's residents." *As headman, I can't let the folks of my village come to harm! On the other hand, I don't want my child to come to harm. But how do I balance my love for a son with my duty to a people? Where do my family responsibilities end and my obligations as a ruler begin?*

"You're not being at all helpful! If you don't like any of my suggestions, why don't you come up with some — of — your — own!" She spat out the last words.

Speaking slowly and choosing his words carefully, the husband replied, "Because I'm at a loss. I'm not sure what to do. The truth is that the Apu-Panaka is just humoring us. He wants us to feel like we're the ones who are deciding K'uchi-Wara's fate. But we're not." *How can I make you understand? The Inkas know that our son's precious to us. It's on account of our love for him that they make us "voluntarily" turn him over as tribute. Because then, when they sacrifice him as a qhapaq hucha, he becomes a symbol of our conquest and lowly position. He becomes a symbol that's etched into our hearts and minds. So they'll never back down from the sacrifice. They can't. That would make them appear weak. It would under-cut their power! But how do I convince you of the truth, my dear, without crushing your spirit? For that matter, how do I convince myself that we have no choice, that in the end we'll have to give up K'uchi-Wara. Because if I let the Inkas take my only child, won't they also take my dignity and joy of life?*

The wife was becoming desperate. "The Apu-Panaka's entourage is small, its members lightly armed. Suppose we call together the men of the village and tell them to bring their weapons. We'll abduct the official, take him hostage! We'll hold him until the Inkas agree to leave our son in peace!"

"Have you lost your mind? You seem to think that we're dealing with a single person, when we're really up against the state. You know what would happen! The state would brand us as rebels, and would send an army to deal with us. They'd burn our houses, sow our gardens with salt, take our herds. They'd kill every one of us. You've heard the stories about how the Inkas treat the corpses of traitors. Once we were dead, they'd knock out our teeth to make necklaces, turn our skin into drumheads, and use our skulls for drinking cups. Is that what you want?"

"I don't care! The Creator gave me the child. He's the most pre-cious thing I've got in the world. He's my happiness, my reason for living! They can't have him. I'd die first!" Her voice rose in pitch as she screamed, "Don't you understand? I — CAN — NOT — GIVE — HIM —

UP! I — WILL — NOT — GIVE — HIM — UP!"

"Of course, I understand! He's my son too! Does the fact that I'm not hysterical mean I love him less?"

"Hysterical? You think I'm hysterical?" The woman became deadly calm. Her voice was cold and flat as she continued, "So, as far as you're concerned, there's nothing we can do to stop the Inkas from claiming K'uchi-Wara?"

"Well, we can't reason with the Apu-Panaka, can't bribe him, can't hide the child from him. And we certainly don't want to take him hostage! What options do we have left?"

"The Inkas leave us no choice. There's only one thing we can do. We're going to cut the child's face. That way, he'll no longer be acceptable as a *qhapaq hucha*."

"What? Are you *mad*? I'm not going to mutilate my son! First, I could never bring myself to do it! Second, from a moral standpoint, that would be no better than handing him over to them."

"At least he'd be alive!"

I remember hearing about a young woman who was going to be sacrificed on an island in Lake Titicaca. When she was first selected as a qhapaq hucha, *a state official examined her body to ensure it had no blemishes. He didn't find any. During the actual sacrifice, though, a priest saw a tiny mole under one of her breasts. He sent her away, saying she was a disgrace. As I recall, the Inkas forced everyone, even her own people, to shun her.* "Yeah, K'uchi-Wara would be alive. But what sort of a life would it be? He'd have a scarlet welt on his face. It would be a mark of shame. And he'd have to carry it for the rest of his days. The Inkas would make certain that no community ever embraced him, that no woman ever married him. He'd be scorned by all. Is that what you want?"

Neither spoke for a long time. Finally she said, "So you've come to the conclusion that there's nothing to be done?"

Gods above, give me the strength to get through this ordeal! "Look—you know that I love our son very much. And that I would do anything to protect him. You also know that I hate the Inkas, who subjugated us and claimed our lands. Even so ..." *I have to be firm, for her sake. I don't want to give her false hope.* "... even so, I don't think that there's anything we can do to prevent him from being taken.

"There is, in fact, only one course of action for us that'll allow us to get through this horrible situation without losing our sanity. There's only one way for us to move forward in our lives without falling into despair. We have to accept the inevitable." *I have to convince her that giving up K'uchi-Wara's for the best. But how do I do that when I'm not completely persuaded myself?* "At the same time, we have to believe. And I mean truly believe that when our child's offered up, he'll be going to a better world. A world where he'll have an easy existence, a world where he'll be happy and free from want."

The mother said nothing. She simply turned from her husband, marched out the door, and slammed it shut.

* * *

The woman stormed out of the house and away from the homestead. As she walked, she kicked a clump of earth as hard as she could, sending it flying. When she reached an open field where she was out of earshot of the house, and where she had a clear view of Qala-Uta, she stopped. Clenching her fists and shaking them at the mountain, she shrieked, "WHY? WHY? WHY? Why have you done this to me, Qala-Uta? Why do you want to take my son from me? Haven't I always treated you with respect? Haven't I always made the proper sacrifices to you? In fact, I've treated you like one of the family, feeding you llama fat and guinea pigs and *chicha*! And this is how you repay me? DAMN YOU! If you don't get the Apu Panaka to change his mind about the boy, I swear that I'll never make another offering to you. For as long as I live! And that I'll destroy the family's shrines dedicated to you. And that I'll make a pilgrimage to your snow-covered slopes and piss on you! How would you like that? Do you hear me?" The woman continued yelling at the peak until she was completely spent.

* * *

The next day, the Apu-Panaka returned to the homestead, where he was received by the father. The latter reluctantly agreed to give up the child. Following Inka norms of behavior, he gave no outward sign of sorrow or remorse for his decision. For his part, the Inka official sealed the deal by presenting the father with exquisite cloth, as required by Andean tradition. The mother was nowhere to be seen.

* * *

The shadows around K'uchi-Wara's house were deepening. In the distance, however, Qala-Uta and its companion peaks were ablaze with color. As the rays of the setting sun reflected off their eternal snows, the three glowed orange and red.

K'uchi-Wara was sitting with Nina and two cousins, Jukumari and Amaru, on the patio. The boys had spent a long day tending their llamas and alpacas. Nina had devoted her day to helping her mother around the house. Her mother was teaching her to cook and weave, skills that would be important when she married.

Nina, who was facing west, smiled. "Look at the mountains!" she exclaimed. "They're so pretty! Did you know I was named for the 'fire' that burns on the peaks in the evening?" Then, turning to K'uchi-Wara, she became more serious. "I've been wondering. How do you feel about becoming a *qhapaq hucha*?"

"Are you kidding? It's great," the boy replied. "I'll finally be able to take a trip." A *real* trip. "The farthest I've ever been from home is the village just downslope from us."

Nina nodded.

"And," he continued, "I'll get a chance to see Cuzco! Addressing Jukumari and Amaru, he said, "If half the stories that Uncle's told us are true, the capital will be amazing. Maybe I'll get to see the king too. He's a living god, you know!"

"I'm so jealous!" Jukumari said excitedly. "I wish I could go with you."

"What do your parents think about you being a *qhapaq hucha*?" Nina asked.

"It's strange, but they don't seem very thrilled about it. Especially my mom. Every time I bring up the subject, she gets upset."

Amaru ("snake"), who was thirteen, said, "Your mom has good reason to be upset. She's going to lose her son."

"What do you mean?" asked Jukumari.

"Do you *babies* have any idea what's going on?" replied Amaru. "Don't you know what's in store for K'uchi-Wara? He's going to be taking a trip, all right. A one-way trip. Then, facing K'uchi-Wara directly, he said, "The Inkas didn't invite you to Cuzco because they're nice people. They mean business. Don't you understand? They want to *sacrifice* you!"

"I'm *not* a baby. And I'm not going to die," stated K'uchi-Wara. "Only old people die. Or sick people. But not guys like me! I'll just be serving the *waqas*, that's all."

"How do you think you get to the land of the *waqas*? Huh?"

Nina said to Amaru, "Why are you being so *mean*?"

"Mean? You call *this* being mean? I call it being honest. But you babies seem to think that being a *qhapaq hucha* is just fun and games. Well, it isn't."

King Wayna Qhapaq addresses the Sun during the festival of the *qhapaq huchas*

Chapter Eight: Cuzco

A slow procession made its way down the mountain. It consisted of K'uchi-Wara, his father and mother, a state dignitary, and several porters. Whenever they walked through a village, they were greeted by the residents, who turned out to see the local celebrity.

At the foot of the mountain, the track that the group followed joined an Inka highway. *What a great road!* K'uchi-Wara thought. *It's much better than the dirt paths we have at home.* It was three paces wide, its edges were marked by low stone walls, and its surface was paved with flagstones.

As the highway headed toward Lake Titicaca, it crossed a series of wide valleys, between which were chains of rolling hills. At one point the party passed a hamlet, little more than a collection of round houses made of mud-bricks. Their conical roofs were thatched with *ichu*.

K'uchi-Wara was with his father, who said, "The people who live here speak Aymara, just like us."

"Oh, no," mumbled the child. "Here it comes–another one of Dad's lessons! I wonder if other kids have to put up with this sort of thing?"

The valley floor near the houses was divided into a dozen or more strips of land. K'uchi-Wara noted that each strip was separated from its neighbor on either side by a line of cone-shaped mounds. The earthen mounds were topped by wisps of grass.

His father spoke: "See these long fields? Each one has been assigned to a particular family by the village headman. The larger the family, the more land it has received. The family members use the land to grow their own food. Some of their produce, though, goes to the headman."

The child looked up at his father. "It's like Wila Nayra then, where the people give you llamas and alpacas. You know, in payment for the work you do."

"Yes," said the man, looking down at his boy and smiling. "So, on occasion you *do* listen to what I tell you!"

Leaving the hamlet behind, the Inka highway skirted some steep hills. K'uchi-Wara, who liked to take in the view while he walked, was astonished to see that from base to summit, all of the hills were ringed by terraces. "Gosh! It must've taken an awful lot of work to build so many terraces!" No sooner had he uttered these words, however, than he realized his mistake. *Oh, no–I've opened myself up to yet another lecture. I've got to learn to keep my mouth shut.*

The boy wasn't wrong. His father immediately said, "You're right, son. It probably took many people laboring for years to construct them. But they're important. They turn what would otherwise be wasteland into productive fields. They hold the soil in place and prevent erosion. They trap rainwater and enable the locals to grow potatoes and other crops."

As he heard these words, K'uchi-Wara noticed some tiny figures working on a faraway terrace. *The farming season's over. So what are those people doing? I suppose they could be repairing the retaining walls or something like that.*

A long ridge extended from the valley floor up to one of the terraced hills. Tracing the gentle slope of the ridge with his eyes, the child was surprised to see three enormous towers on it. While two of them were cylindrical in shape, the third was square. Even from a distance, he could tell they were made from large and skillfully cut stones. This time he was genuinely interested when he pointed at the towers and asked, "What are *those*?"

To the boy's surprise, his father scowled. Then the man looked around until he was able to locate the state dignitary, who was walking some distance ahead. Dropping his voice, he almost growled, "*Those* are Inka *chullpas.* The empire entombs its honored dead in them. By building them, the Inkas have put their mark on *our* land. It's their way of claiming it!"

K'uchi-Wara could hear the bitterness in his father's voice. Thus he remained silent, at least for a little while.

The highway, which was approaching Lake Titicaca, forded a silver stream by way of a low footbridge. The footbridge had been placed at the point where the stream widened and its waters slowed. Its piers consisted of boulders that had been hewn to give them a rough rectangular shape. The piers supported large slabs of stone. Ambling over the structure, the child peered into the clear water. He stopped, puzzled. The streambed appeared to be covered with hundreds of white cobblestones. *How odd.* He turned to his father and said, "What are those things?"

His father glanced over the edge of the footbridge. "It's white *chuño.* People in these parts soak their potatoes in cold water for several weeks. It preserves them. And it turns them white."

K'uchi-Wara was glad to hear that the bite was gone from his father's voice.

The party walked all day. Towards evening they reached the shores of Lake Titicaca, where they decided to stop for the night. So they located a *tampu.* This small rectangular lodging-house, which had been built by the Inkas, had walls that were made of fieldstones held together with a mortar of adobe. Its steeply pitched roof was thatched. It was maintained by the local populace. Although not luxurious, it was nonetheless comfortable, especially when compared to what the family was used to.

At dinnertime, the caretaker, a kindly old man, fetched a large blanket from the building. He spread it out on the patio and invited K'uchi-Wara, his parents, and the state dignitary to sit. Then he brought them bowls of fish stew and plates of roasted *uqa,* a highland tuber.

K'uchi-Wara tasted the stew. He told the old man, "Mmm, I love this dish! I've never had fish before. Where does it come from?"

The caretaker gave him a toothless smile. He replied, "I'm glad you like it. We get our fish from the lake."

The group resumed their journey in the morning. They followed the Inka road, which hugged the southwestern margin of Lake Titicaca. K'uchi-Wara happened to be walking near the state dignitary when they crossed a shallow bay on a causeway. The child, who was interested in almost everything, wanted to ask the man about the structure. He hesitated, though. Not only was he a little shy, but somewhat leery about talking to an Inka official, especially after seeing his father's response on the previous day to the Inka burial towers. Finally his curiosity got the better of him. He blurted out, "How did your people build this thing?"

K'uchi-Wara didn't know how the man would react to the question. *Will he scold me? Will hail shoot from his eyes like a* qoa? The dignitary casually turned to face the boy. He said, "Well, we had a work gang bring a large amount of fill here. They dumped the fill into the bay, leveled it off, and paved the top of it. The causeway allows people and llama caravans to traverse this swampy area safely." And that was that.

Walking along the structure, the child stopped. He looked out over the boundless lake. *I've never seen anything like this, except maybe in my dreams.* As the day was warm and sunny, and as there was no wind, its surface was glassy smooth. At the far horizon, the azure of the water touched the cobalt of the air: lake mirroring sky, sky mirroring lake. When he glanced behind in the direction from which they had come, he saw the majestic form of Qala-Uta. It was an immense stone block crowned with white. On either side of it were its brother peaks. *Was Amaru right? Is this the last I'll see of my homeland?* Leaving the causeway and continuing up the road, the high mountains disappeared behind low hills.

After following the shore of Lake Titicaca for a while, the Inka highway veered toward the northwest, and headed directly for Cuzco.

* * *

K'uchi-Wara wasn't sure what to expect from the Inkas or from their capital. At home, sitting by the hearth after dinner, his uncle had recounted stories about the Inkas and their fabulous wealth. And he had spun yarns about Cuzco. He claimed that the city was full of magnificent temples and palaces and plazas. He once told his enthralled audience, K'uchi-Wara and his cousins, their faces lit by the glow of lamps, that there were buildings made of stone blocks that were higher than a man. Yet they fit together so perfectly, you couldn't insert a thin knife between them. He also described the Golden Enclosure. This temple supposedly had a garden where everything was made of precious metals: Among the rows of golden corn were lizards and insects of silver. Off to the side grazed life-sized llamas fashioned from beaten gold, while overhead flew silver hummingbirds. *But are these stories really true?*

The closer the family got to the city, the busier the road became. Whereas at the start of their trip they had been almost alone, now they were part of a growing crowd. Everyone was trying to get to the capital for the festival of the *qhapaq huchas*. It was held but every four years.

By the time K'uchi-Wara and his parents actually entered Cuzco, the crowd had swelled to a large and boisterous throng. The boy saw other kids his age, each of whom was at the center of a cluster of people. *I'll bet that they're qhapaq huchas, just like me. They'll probably be taking part in the celebration too.* It appeared that they were accompanied by their parents. Within many groups there also was a man or woman, usually older, who was more elaborately dressed than the others. *I wonder if those are the kurakas of the regions where the kids come from? I'm lucky because Dad's my kuraka.* There were commoners as well.

The boy saw eight men, who were part of a large group, bearing a litter on their burly shoulders. On top of the litter sat a big rock. It was carved with the images of a man, a woman, and little snakes and toads. It was encrusted with a reddish-brown substance.

K'uchi-Wara came alongside one of the bearers and asked, "What's that you're carrying?"

"Our village's main *waqa*."

"Where's your village?"

"On the western shore of Lake Titicaca."

"Really? That's not far from where I live. In my village, though, we honor a high mountain instead of a stone. But we couldn't bring the mountain with us. What's that reddish crud on your *waqa*?"

"It's blood. The dried blood of sacrificed llamas."

It had taken the child and his parents weeks to walk to Cuzco. Although excited to be there, they were tired from the long journey. So the dignitary who had accompanied them took them directly to the place where they would be staying, located outside the city core.

"Amazing!" K'uchi-Wara said to the dignitary when he first saw the building. "I can't believe you're housing us in a palace." By this time, the boy had gotten used to the man, and was no longer shy around him.

"Huh? You think *this* is a palace? Why, it's nothing but a *kallanka*."

The *kallanka* was a long rectangular hall. It had a stone foundation, and adobe walls that were plastered with fine mud and painted a cheery shade of yellow. Its three doors were trapezoidal, with double jambs. The gabled roof was thatched with thick bundles of straw whose edges were perfectly cut.

The dignitary led K'uchi-Wara and his parents through one of the doors and into the hall. The inside was like a barracks, without internal divisions. It was designed to accommodate large numbers of people. Along each side wall, the boy saw a lengthy row of sleeping platforms. As the dignitary explained, they were assigned, one to a family, based on status and ethnic background. "We want you to feel at home here. Thus we've grouped your family with other lower-class nobles from the same province. Two communal meals will be served each day on the patio."

K'uchi-Wara and his parents spent a restful night, despite their unfamiliar surroundings. Early the next day, they were met by an elderly man, who stood proud and erect, despite his advanced years. He spoke Quechua with perfect e - nun - ci - á - tion: "Hello, my name is Samin ('fortunate'), and I will be your guide. As you know, we call our empire Tawantin-Suyu ('land of the four quarters'). The name refers to the fact that the state is divided into four parts. You people are from Qulla-Suyu, the southeastern quarter, are you not?"

"Yes," replied the boy and his father in unison. The mother said nothing.

"Very good. Welcome to Cuzco. Let me start by telling you a little about our capital. Only twenty thousand people live in the city core. They include members of the royal family, aristocrats, high priests, and important bureaucrats. Most of the inhabitants live in the neighborhoods that ring the city's hub."

Cuzco had been built within and around the sides of a bowl-shaped valley. The family's *kallanka* was situated high on a south-facing slope. So, to reach the center of town, Samin led the trio down a long flight of stone steps. Approaching the valley floor, they entered a maze of cobbled streets. The old gentleman, however, seemed to know exactly where he was going. He took them through a narrow alley between two large buildings. Indicating the structure on their left, he said, "This is the palace of King Inka Roka."

In the middle of the palace wall, the child saw a massive and irregularly shaped stone. Its twelve sides abutted eleven other stones. He ran his hand over the central stone, feeling how flat it was. As his fingers followed the smoothly beveled edge down to the sunken joint, he noted that it fit perfectly with the next stone, whose edges were also beveled. "*Añañau*–astounding! Look Mom, look Dad! See how the wall is made up of stones of all shapes and sizes?"

"Yes, we see," said his mother, who was not very enthusiastic about things Inka.

"How was it built?" K'uchi-Wara asked their guide. "Uncle told me that some of the Inkas are powerful sorcerers. Their magic is so great, all they have to do is order the rocks to come together. And sure enough, the rocks follow their will, and form a wall!"

The old man chuckled, shaking his head. "Actually, tens of thousands of guestworkers come to Cuzco every year. They provide the labor for large construction projects, such as the building of palace walls."

Then they walked to a large open space in the middle of the city that was surrounded by buildings. The great plaza was nearly deserted. As K'uchi-Wara was marveling at its size, Samin told him, "This is the

Awqay-Pata. You will be coming here tomorrow for the *qhapaq hucha* festival."

From the Awqay-Pata, they headed southeast. After several blocks, they came to a wall of finely cut grey stone. It curved gracefully and leaned inward toward the top. When they stopped in front of it, K'uchi-Wara blurted out, "Look how this wall is made of identical blocks. It's completely different from Inka Roka's wall!"

"Ahem," their guide cleared his throat. "As I was about to say, here we have the Golden Enclosure, the holiest temple in the realm. It consists of eight chapels grouped around a square courtyard. The chapels are sheathed in plates of pure gold and silver. They house the statues of the most important gods. Unfortunately I cannot show them to you due to their sacredness."

"Have *you* ever seen them?" K'uchi-Wara asked with wide-eyed wonder.

"Good heavens, no," came the reply, each word pronounced with equal clarity. "Only the king, his family, and the high priests can visit the chapels. To violate their sanctity is to invite death."

"Uncle says there's a garden in the Golden Enclosure where everything's made of gold and silver. Is that true?"

"Yes, it is."

From the Golden Enclosure, they wandered north, admiring the architecture as they went. The boy noticed that many of the buildings were similar to the *kallanka*: they had adobe walls that were plastered and painted vivid colors such as red, yellow, or blue. Most of the structures were elaborately thatched. "What would happen if a roof caught fire? I imagine that the flames would jump from building to building. Pretty soon the *whole* city'd be burning!"

The blood drained from their guide's face as he stared blankly at the child. Recovering his composure somewhat, he said, "Fortunately, Inti, guardian of the empire, would *never* allow such a thing to happen."

The festival of the *qhapaq huchas* began the next morning. K'uchi-Wara and the other sacrificial victims, their parents, the *kurakas*, and the commoners took part in a procession to the main plaza. As this parade wound its way through the streets, the local populace, who had turned out for the event, cheered. *"WAQE!"* they shouted. "HURRAY!"

Reaching the Awqay-Pata, only the sacrificial victims could enter. Hence fifty children lined up single file and marched into the great open space. K'uchi-Wara was sixth in line. As he walked, he felt his stomach flutter as if it were full of butterflies. *Why am I so nervous? I guess it's because I don't really know what's going to happen today.* To take his mind off his worries, he began to look around. Then he noticed that the perimeter of the square was packed with thousands of spectators. *I've never seen so many people! And all their attention's focused on me!* His legs began to shake. It was some time before he was able to calm himself.

The victims stood at attention near the center of the Awqay-Pata. A herald announced in a loud clear voice the arrival of the Inka gods. The crowd grew quiet in anticipation. Four strong men, walking in lockstep, carried a litter into the square. On top of the litter, K'uchi-Wara could see the image of the Sun god. *Inti's statue is terrific! I bet it's made of gold. And it looks like a boy with ... what are those strange things sticking out of his head? Solar rays? I like the snakes wrapped around his arms, and the puma heads sticking out from between his legs.* The Sun god's image was adorned with ear-spools, a chest ornament, and a headband. Behind the litter came Inti's male priests and attendants. They were richly dressed.

The four litter-bearers walked to the middle of the plaza. They set their burden down. Meanwhile one of the attendants placed a small bench on the ground, which he covered with an elaborate cloth. Then the priests carefully lifted the Sun's statue from the litter and set it on the bench.

The second image to be carried into the Awqay-Pata was that of Mama-Killa, Inti's wife and sister. *Mother-Moon's statue seems to be made of silver. It's about the same size and shape as Nina. And all the goddess's priests and attendants are women.* After Mama-Killa's image came those of Thunder-Lightning, Mother-Earth, and Mother-Sea. Before long, there was a line of benches, each of which supported a god. The gods faced the children, the children faced the gods.

Next the herald announced the arrival of the Inka kings. *What does he mean by "kings"? I thought there was only one ruler at a time.* K'uchi-Wara did not have long to wait for an answer. Once again, four men, walking in lockstep, bore a litter into the square. On the litter sat a king. His back was perfectly straight. He held his head high, and appeared to be staring into the far distance. The man wore fine garments and beautiful adornments. The litter was followed by several priests and servants.

As the litter passed him, K'uchi-Wara stared at the ruler. *Why isn't he moving? He seems to be frozen.*

Sensing his confusion, the boy standing beside K'uchi-Wara whispered in his ear, "That's Pacha-Kuti's mummy. He was the greatest of all the Inka kings."

K'uchi-Wara nodded. *Mummy? He's so well preserved, he looks like he's still alive. Hold on, did that kid say Pacha-Kuti? He's the ruler who conquered our people! He's the one who took our lands!* As these thoughts ran through his head, the boy reflexively clenched his jaw and fists.

Pacha-Kuti's litter was followed by nine others, each of which bore the mummy of a past king. Like the statues of the gods, the mummies were set on benches, all in a line. They too faced the children, while the children faced them. Servants took their places behind the kings. In their hands the servants held parasols of brightly colored feathers that they used to keep the sunlight off their masters' faces. They would slowly shift their positions as the sun inched across the sky during the course of the day.

After the rulers of old came the present one. The herald started to announce the king's entrance into the plaza. But his voice was drowned out by the roar of the crowd along the perimeter. "WAYNA QHAPAQ! WAYNA QHAPAQ!" A tall well-built man came striding into the Awqay-Pata. K'uchi-Wara wasn't sure what to do. *Is it okay to stare at a "living god"? Maybe I should look down.* Eventually his curiosity overcame his unease, however, and he turned his gaze toward the man.

Hmm, what makes him so special? He looks strong, though nothing out of the ordinary. Dad could probably beat him in an arm-wrestling contest. Maybe it's the clothes that make the king. His tunic's pretty fancy. The front of the garment was divided into little squares, each of which bore a geometric design. It was brightly colored: red, blue, white, green, yellow, black, and orange. *It appears to be very soft; it's probably woven from vicuña wool.* Over the tunic, and partly obscuring it, was a mantle. *Or is it his wealth that makes him so mighty?* The man wore enormous ear-spools inlaid with precious stones, a gold bracelet, and other costly adornments. *Uncle says that to rule, you have to have the right symbols of office.* Circling the king's head was a multi-hued band from which hung the most important royal insignia, a scarlet fringe. The fringe was as wide as a person's hand, and covered part of the forehead. In Wayna Qhapaq's right hand he held another symbol of office, a mace with a long wooden handle and a star-shaped head of gold.

The king made his way to the statues of the gods, all in a row. Standing before them, he bowed. He honored the mummies of his ancestors in the same way. An attendant carried a low stool made of gold into the square. He set it down at the head of the long line of gods and mummies. Wayna Qhapaq took a seat.

A parade of important Inkas entered the Awqay-Pata and filed past the ruler, gods, and mummies. First came the "captains" of the army. They were dressed in the typical Inka style, except that they wore helmets on their heads. The helmets were decorated with ornamental fringes and plumes. Many soldiers had large disks of gold or silver hanging from their necks. In their hands they carried spears, slings, bright banners, halberds, square shields, and star-headed maces. *They sure look tough. I wouldn't want to mess with them.* Next came members of the Inka nobility. One of them wore a headdress made from the feathers of Amazonian birds. *Añañau! How colorful and beautiful!* Another had a tunic covered with silver spangles, which were arranged on the garment like the scales on a fish's body. *Every time the guy moves, his tunic flashes sunlight right in my eyes. It's blinding.*

When the parade of Inkas ended, a priest took charge of the fifty *qhapaq huchas*. He directed K'uchi-Wara and the other boys and girls to go before the king and kneel. They had to kneel before the gods and mummies too. Then the priest led them twice around the Awqay-Pata. Directly in front of K'uchi-Wara strode a tall confident boy. *He seems very sure of himself. And just look at his clothing.* The boy wore a short tunic, a mantle, and sandals. What attracted K'uchi-Wara's attention, though, was the wide feathered collar around his neck. *I wonder where he's from? Too bad Jukumari and Nina couldn't be here with me! I miss them. It'd be nice to share these strange sights and sounds with them.*

Completing the second circuit of the square, the victims were told to stop in front of Wayna Qhapaq. As they did so, he rose from his stool. He raised his arms as if to embrace them, and said in a deep and pleasing voice, "Greetings *qhapaq huchas*. I welcome you to Cuzco."

The queen and two of her daughters appeared. *They're the prettiest women I've ever seen! And their fine clothing makes them look even more beautiful.* The queen's attire consisted of a brightly colored, ankle-length dress that was fastened at each shoulder by a large gold pin. It was bound at the waist by a sash. The dress accentuated the slender form of her body. Over her shoulders she wore a mantle, which, like the dress, was secured with a gold pin. On her feet were sandals. Her long hair, parted in the middle, hung loosely down her back. It was jet-black and shiny with an iridescent quality like a raven's wings. The daughters had similar clothing and hairstyles.

The princesses carried golden pitchers containing what K'uchi-Wara assumed to be *chicha*. One of them filled a gold cup handed to her by an assistant. She gave it to the king, who said, "I toast you, Inti." He drank. A priest, playing the part of the Sun, reciprocated by draining a cup in honor of the ruler. The king then toasted each of his mummified ancestors, who likewise reciprocated through their priests.

Wayna Qhapaq stood tall and regal. He faced Inti's golden statue. A profound silence fell over the square. He adjusted the mantle on his shoulders, and cleared his throat. He said in his rich voice, "Lord Sun, my father, I formally offer you the lives of these Chosen Ones. I do so in the name of your children, the Inkas." As he spoke, he swept his right arm in a broad arc that took in all of the *qhapaq huchas*.

K'uchi-Wara wasn't sure why. Perhaps it was the words themselves or some quality in the king's voice. Maybe it was the hush of the crowd or the dramatic arm gesture. Whatever the reason, this small event sent chills up and down his spine. He thought back to what his cousin Amaru had told him: *"The Inkas didn't invite you to Cuzco because they're nice. They mean business. They want to sacrifice you!"*

Minor priests brought several dozen snow-white llamas to the middle of the Awqay-Pata. K'uchi-Wara had heard that because of their color, these llamas were sacred to Inti. As the boy and the other *qhapaq huchas* watched, a high priest grabbed the head of the lead animal, pointed it toward the Sun's image, and slit its throat. The rest of the llamas began a terrified bleating. The pathetic sound rekindled K'uchi-Wara's fear. Their din compounded the pounding of his heart. *Is this what's going to happen to me?* The priest sacrificed the remaining animals, one by one, while praying:

> "Oh, Inti, who gives us night and day, preserve the Lord Inka, your son. Grant that he may be victorious over his enemies, and may always be a conqueror. Give him peace and prosperity. Keep him safe from harm. Do not cut his days short!

> "Oh, Sun, who gives us light and heat, multiply the fruits of the earth so men do not suffer from hunger or want. Make the corn grow tall and strong and plentiful. Preserve the crops from hail and frost!

> "Oh, Inti, who gives us dawn and twilight, shine upon your children, the Inkas. Grant that they may always be conquerors, for this is why you created them. Give them peace and health and prosperity. Do not cut their days short."

An enormous bonfire was lit. The minor priests hacked the bodies of the llamas to pieces, tossing them into the flames along with baskets of coca leaves and other offerings. *Atatau! The smell of burning wool is horrible. I think I'm going to throw up!*

Musicians carrying heavy drums entered the square. They were followed by men holding trumpets made from giant seashells, and by singers. As the drummers took up a slow and steady beat, the choir began to chant. Their words were accentuated by the trumpeters. A line of dancers, both men and women, appeared and started to cross the plaza with funereal steps. They took a long time to reach the far side.

The solemn rites ended at sunset. By then K'uchi-Wara felt mentally exhausted. An Inka official reunited him with his parents at the *kallanka*. Seeing him, the boy's mother knelt to give him a big hug.

"What's that for?" the child asked.

"I haven't seen you all day, and have missed you," she replied in Quechua. Then switching to Aymara, she added, "Besides, I don't trust the Inkas! I was afraid they'd take you away. And that we'd never see you again."

Now that he was with his mother and father, the boy was reassured that everything was okay. He felt comforted by their presence. The pangs of fear he had experienced earlier in the day had vanished. "Oh, Mom," K'uchi-Wara said smiling, "you make everything sound so dramatic! Did you see the ceremony? Were you watching when I stood before the king?"

"Yeah, we saw that part of the ceremony," responded his father. "But the crowd kept surging and pushing in front of us. So we didn't always have the best view. For some reason, the Inkas made us leave the square in the afternoon. That's why we weren't sure what had happened to you. How did it feel to be a *qhapaq hucha*?"

K'uchi-Wara thought about the question, but was unable to answer it. The truth was he didn't know how to put his experience into words. Thinking back on the day, he saw it as a kaleidoscope of constantly shifting colors and forms. His mind was awhirl with a hodgepodge of images. Some were more concrete and permanently fixed in his memory, while others were hazy and already being forgotten.

During the rites, he had felt a wide range of emotions. He remembered being intrigued at one point, bored shortly thereafter. He had been delighted one moment, horrified the next. Although he could make sense of some of his feelings, many were confusing. A part of him was exhilarated, having shared in the collective thrill of being a *qhapaq hucha*. Also, this day had held a great deal of adventure for him. Yet another part of him wanted nothing more than to go home and resume his life as a herder. When he thought about what was to come, he felt very excited. But there also was an element of fear. The fear made him want to bury his face between his mother's breasts and cry.

That night, K'uchi-Wara, his mother, and father attended a feast. The boy stuffed himself with all kinds of delicacies, not all of which he recognized. Most of them were delicious, though. And he tried *chicha* and coca for the first time. *They're awful! Corn-beer tastes sour, while coca leaves are bitter and make my tongue go numb.*

Several days later, all the *qhapaq huchas*, parents, and *kurakas* who were native to Qulla-Suyu were brought together for another ceremony. It was presided over by a high lord. He was in charge of the quarter's internal affairs and sat on a council that advised King Wayna Qhapaq. He presented K'uchi-Wara and the other male victims with special emblems of nobility. Although the boy was too young to wear a black headband, he nonetheless got one. He also received a condor-feather headdress, a double-crescent pendant, a silver bracelet, and moccasins, just like the ones worn by his father. *Now that I have all this grownup stuff, I'm a man. If only Nina could see me. She'd be so impressed!*

When the festival ended, many *qhapaq huchas* were offered up at sacred sites around Cuzco, including in the Golden Enclosure. Those who were not immediately sacrificed appeared before the Willka-Kamayuq. As K'uchi-Wara's father explained, this royal official was familiar with the most important *waqas* in the *suyus*. The *waqas* included mountains, lakes, springs, hills, stones, trees, temples, palaces, forts, shrines, and idols. It was the Willka-Kamayuq who decided where to send each victim.

K'uchi-Wara felt small and vulnerable. He walked across an open patio, through a trapezoidal door, and into a room. Despite it being bright and sunny outside, the room was dimly lit. It took a little while for his eyes to adjust to the darkness. When they did, he saw the Willka-Kamayuq seated on a stool against the back wall. *Where will he send me? Where? Where? Where?* As this question went through his mind, the child realized that he was almost as nervous as when he had stood before the king. His palms were sweaty, his legs shaky, and the walls seemed to close in on him. To get a grip on himself, he wiped his hands on his tunic. He clenched his fists by his side, locked his knees so his legs wouldn't buckle, and took several deep breaths. *This guy's going to decide my future. I hope he chooses a* waqa *that's far away, so it'll take a long time to get there. I'd prefer to start serving the gods later rather than sooner!* Just then, he became aware of a voice. It was that of the Willka-Kamayuq.

"Um ... sorry sir ... did you say something?"

"Yes! I was speaking to you!" The man sounded annoyed. "Are you the boy from the Lake Titicaca area? The one who's been called the 'darling of his mountain-*waqa*'?"

"Gulp ... I guess so."

"Okay, then it would make sense to assign you to a peak. One in your own quarter."

The Willka-Kamayuq rose from his seat, raised his right arm, and declared with great solemnity, "I hereby designate you for sacrifice on Titi-Urqu ('lead mountain'), in the newly conquered lands to the south." He then turned to another man, who was sitting on a lower stool. The man held a cord in his hands. From this long cord dangled shorter cords, each a different color. The Willka-Kamayuq commanded, "Keeper of the *khipus*, finish recording the information on the *qhapaq huchas* who we're sending to Qulla-Suyu."

"Yes, sir," said the Khipu-Kamayuq, as he began to tie little knots in various cords. The final one was placed at the end of the last and shortest cord. It represented the number "two." It told him that two children were going to the southern extreme of Tawantin-Suyu. Although K'uchi-

Wara did not know it, reaching these distant lands would involve a long journey of many months. A journey that would be difficult and fraught with danger.

Waman, the junior priest, pays homage to Putina Volcano

Chapter Nine: The Volcanoes

After a week-long stay, K'uchi-Wara left Cuzco. He was accompanied by an entourage: his parents, a state official, priests, attendants, and llama-train drivers. As they made their way through the Inka capital, they were applauded by the local people, who lined the streets. Other groups of *qhapaq huchas* were also leaving. When they reached the stone markers indicating the city limits and started walking among grassy hills, the child was reminded of his homeland and felt more relaxed. They followed the main road south. It headed toward what is today the city of Arequipa.

Another boy, who appeared to be about six years old, came up beside K'uchi-Wara. *"Peinas unam,"* he said. Then switching to Quechua, he asked, "Do you know what that means?"

"No," replied the eight-year-old.

"It means 'good morning' in Mochica. That's what we speak at home. But the Inkas made us learn Quechua, just like you."

"What's your name?"

"Qispi ('crystal'). Do you know why my parents call me that?"

"No."

"Because I'm pure. And nice to look at, just like a crystal. Anyway, that's what my mom tells me. And that's why the Inkas chose me to be a *qhapaq hucha*."

K'uchi-Wara took a good look at the kid. Regardless of the six-year-old's name, he was *not* the most handsome child in the world. He was short, thin, and gawky. His face was long, his eyes large, his jaw narrow. Yet his teeth seemed so outsized it was a wonder that all of them could fit in his mouth. His stringy black hair reached his shoulders. *Wa!* the eight-year-old thought in astonishment. *If he's the best the Inkas have to offer their gods, then they're in trouble.* But what he said was, "I'm K'uchi-Wara."

"*Ahau!* That's a funny name!"

"You think so? Well, I don't. Maybe it sounds strange to you because it's Aymara."

"Is that what your family speaks?"

"Yes. Where do you come from?"

"Chinchay-Suyu. My dad's the *kuraka* of a large valley in the north-west quarter. We grow lots of corn, beans, and peanuts."

"Do you live near the ocean?" asked the eight-year-old, suddenly taking an interest in the conversation. "I've always wanted to visit the ocean. But I've never had the chance." He had only seen the Mother of All Waters in his dreams.

"Not far from it. But since I grew up near the shore, I'm having trouble breathing up here."

"*What?*" exclaimed K'uchi-Wara with exaggerated disbelief. "This isn't so high. My village sits wayyyy up on a mountain! If you ever came for a visit, you'd probably faint from the thin air. But I want to hear more about the sea. What's it like to look across endless blue water?"

* * *

Each member of the entourage had a particular job to do. K'uchi-Wara's mother and father—as well as Qispi's parents, who had joined the party—were supposed to make sure that their son stayed happy and safe. And that he remained healthy. The Inka official dealt with logistics, and acted as the group's liaison with the state. It was his duty to see that everything ran smoothly on the trip. As he was fond of telling the rest of the party, he was of noble blood. The three attendants were commoners. They were charged not only with helping the official, but with providing labor for odd jobs. The trio of llama-drivers took care of the animals in the caravan. Day in and day out they also packed and unpacked the personal effects of the party, the gear, the food, and the firewood.

Two priests were assigned to the group. One was called Waman ("falcon"), which is a common name in Quechua. Waman was tall and lean. He had an oval face topped by a patch of black hair cropped so short that it stood up like the bristles of a brush. Being kindly and good-natured, he usually had a smile on his lips and little crinkly lines around his eyes. Not so the other priest. Old and stern, he never bore a cheerful expression. As the children were unable to learn his name, they called him the "Old One." The Old One was wiry and surprisingly strong for a man his age. His weather-beaten face was distinct with its deep-set almond-shaped eyes, prominent cheeks, aquiline nose, and cleft chin. Sometimes his visage seemed so hard and impassive it was almost as if it had been cast in bronze and given a deep brown patina.

* * *

The Inka official explained to the rest of the entourage that as a *qhapaq hucha* traveled from the capital to his designated *waqa*, he was supposed to follow a straight line. From a practical standpoint, though, this wasn't always possible. If K'uchi-Wara were to take the most direct route from Cuzco to central Chile, for example, he would end up in the ocean. To solve this problem, his course of travel would be divided into sections. Then, to the extent possible, he would follow a beeline within each section.

K'uchi-Wara and company kept to the royal highway as much as they could. The boys always walked barefooted. The shoes that the eight-year-old had received from the lord of Qulla-Suyu were for ceremonial use, so he could not wear them. During a typical day, they traveled about two and a half *tupus* (twelve miles), the maximum distance a llama train can cover.

As the party made its way south, its members would form little cliques. Within a clique, the people walked together, conversing and enjoying each other's company. Each one moved at its own pace. It might remain stable for hours, as measured by the movement of the sun, or even days. Eventually, though, the clique would break up. Sometimes people ran out of things to say, or they started getting on one another's nerves, or they simply wanted a change. When this happened, the members separated, then came together to form new cliques.

As a rule, K'uchi-Wara's parents traveled together, as did Qispi's. The Old One walked with the Inka official, with Waman, or by himself. The eight-year-old, who wanted to assert his independence, did not always like being seen in the company of his parents. So he often traveled with Waman or the llama drivers. Or he and Qispi, being energetic kids, would take off down the Inka highway, leaving the rest of the party behind.

* * *

K'uchi-Wara walked abreast of the llama drivers, trying to communicate with them. Although they spoke Quechua, they had thick "country" accents, which made understanding them difficult. The boy felt a special kinship with them since he had spent most of his life herding llamas and alpacas.

"How many animals are there in the train?" he asked a driver.

"'Bout thirty."

"How old are they?"

"'Tween three and ten."

"Are they all geldings?"

"For the most part."

"Well, they're beautiful animals. And they seem healthy. You obviously take good care of them."

"Thanks," said the man, an odd grin on his face.

K'uchi-Wara had the feeling that the driver wasn't taking him very seriously. Then he realized why. "You must find it strange to be complimented by an eight-year-old."

"That's true."

"I guess it's especially strange because my compliments have to do with your job, which you've probably been doing since before I was born!"

The man just smiled.

"Do your animals *hum*?"

"Hum?"

"Yes," said the boy. "You know, make a humming sound when they're happy."

"Oh, I see what you mean. We call it singing. Yeah, they sing when they're grazing."

In the silence that followed, K'uchi-Wara studied the packtrain's lead llama, which the other animals followed naturally. It had a light brown coat with big black patches. Its ears were pierced and decorated with large red tassels. It wore a silver bell around its neck, which tinkled as it walked.

"What's his name?" the child asked, pointing at the animal.

"I call him Illapa. You know, after the Rain-god."

"Why?"

"'Cause the black patches on his back remind me of rain clouds, that's why," the man said, chuckling.

Without warning, a heavily-laden gelding plopped down in the middle of the road. It brought the whole packtrain to a halt. One of the llama-drivers ran up to it and started whipping its rump with a sling. To no avail, the animal refused to budge.

"What's wrong with it?" K'uchi-Wara asked the driver beside him.

"Nothing out of the ordinary," the man replied. "Gelding's just tired, that's all. As I'm sure you know, they can't carry much weight. And they tire easily. But not to worry, we have plenty of animals in reserve. Now, if you'll 'scuse me . . ."

The man walked to the back of the packtrain, where there were ten llamas without loads. Choosing one, he led it to where the weary gelding still sat in the road. The gelding carried two large woolen sacks, each of which weighed about thirty-five pounds. The sacks were hoisted from its back and hitched to the back of the fresh animal. They were placed on opposite sides for balance. Then the driver shouted, "USHA, USHA, USHA!" The lead llama started walking, and the packtrain continued on its way.

* * *

The Old One walked in a solemn manner, his face cold and impassive. Every once in a while, assuming the role of royal cheerleader, he led the group in a chorus of shouts: "INTI, OUR FATHER—GIVE THE KING PEACE—KEEP HIM IN HEALTH—GRANT HIM LONG LIFE!" Several times the procession met peasants on the road coming in the opposite direction. The priest always yelled at them, "*QHAPAQ HUCHAS*! Sacred *qhapaq huchas!* Get down on the ground!" The people had to prostrate themselves and avert their eyes until the company had passed.

* * *

K'uchi-Wara was thrilled to be on the road. *I didn't know that the empire was so big or that it had so many different types of terrain. I like walking along the royal highway and watching the landscape change.*

The party ascended a broad valley carpeted with *ichu*. Down the middle of it flowed a lazy stream that sparkled in the morning light. Here and there, the stream was flanked by wide bars of gravel and cobbles. As the day progressed and the group moved along, the valley narrowed. The walls on either side rose up and became steeper. Lofty hills appeared, which were capped by rugged turrets of stone that looked like sugar loaves. In this part of the valley, where the stream was more confined, it ran swifter and straighter. Its waters were white with foam as they danced among the boulders.

The narrow valley turned to the west. "Look!" K'uchi-Wara said excitedly to Qispi. "Look at that mountain lake."

The lake, which had come into view as the valley had opened up again, sat in a bowl, surrounded by snow-streaked peaks. Rising out of its azure waters were hillocks covered with yellow grasses. As there wasn't a breath of wind, the lake mirrored a blue sky with puffy white clouds. When the boys reached its rocky shore, the eight-year-old grabbed his friend's arm. He pointed out in the water. "See the birds?" A flock of ducks paddled leisurely past them, making ripples that ruined the perfect reflection of the sky. The ducks had black heads, chestnut colored bodies, and baby-blue bills. Occasionally one of them would stick its head underwater, whereupon its stiff tail feathers would shoot straight up in the air. "Ajajay," the children laughed.

Several days after passing the highland lake, the Inka highway took K'uchi-Wara and his entourage into a deep gorge. This experience was not only alien, but completely unsettling, to the boy. For as the stone-paved road made its way along the steep side of the gorge, it cut through what he considered to be astonishingly thick vegetation: a hopeless tangle of stems, stalks, shoots, sprigs, branches, leaves, twigs, and trunks, forming what seemed an impenetrable wall. He felt claustrophobic as he ducked under a canopy of boughs and brushed aside some long tendrils that hung in front of his face.

"Dad?"

"Yeah," said his father, who was walking just ahead of him.

"Where did all this greenery come from? Why's this valley so different from the others that we've seen?"

His father stopped. He turned around and faced his son. "You know, I'm not really sure. I suppose it's because this place gets a lot of rain."

They continued. The royal road kept fairly level, but curved in and out as it followed the contours of the gorge. K'uchi-Wara's father stopped again.

"What is it, Dad?"

"*Wa*, the road's gone!"

"Huh? What do you mean?"

"See for yourself."

Coming alongside his father, the child saw that, indeed, the Inka high-way had vanished.

The man went on, "It looks like there's been a landslide. As I said, it probably rains a lot in these parts during the wet season. With all the rain, the earth becomes soaked, which leads to landslides. Every dry season, the Inkas probably have to rebuild the road. The question is, do we continue? Or do we wait for the rest of the group?"

K'uchi-Wara gazed at the long slope ahead. It was all loose rock and soil and debris. It was completely devoid of vegetation. Someone, though, had made a narrow path across the tenuous surface.

"*Way!*" he replied nervously. "We have to cross it sometime. I guess that now's as good a time as any."

"Okay, we'll go now. But we'll take it slowly and cautiously." With that, the father walked out onto the slope. K'uchi-Wara followed.

The boy stepped as gingerly as possible: *left foot, right foot, left foot, right foot, be very careful, stay alert!* Unfortunately the path wasn't quite flat, but tilted slightly downslope, so that he was always a little off balance. To make matters worse, every once in a while the child would set his foot down, only to have the loose soil collapse beneath it. Then he would be left teetering and in danger of tumbling into the gorge. Still he continued.

K'uchi-Wara had made it about three-quarters of the way across the slope without mishap. *Just a little bit to go!* A high-pitched SHREIK suddenly rent the air. The terrible sound came from behind the boy. As he jerked around to see who or what had made it, he was thrown off balance. And nearly fell. He recovered, however, just in time to watch something go rolling down the steep incline: he saw flailing legs, then a long neck and head, then the flailing legs again. It was a llama, heavily laden with supplies. Picking up speed, the animal triggered a small avalanche of rocks, and left a cloud of dust in its wake. Finally it was lost to view. Although shaken, the child finished the crossing.

Another time, as K'uchi-Wara and Qispi walked along the stone-paved road together, it led them up onto a plateau. The sun had passed its zenith, and the afternoon promised to be warm. On either side of them were fields of low grasses, brown and dry. The grasses rustled eerily in the breeze.

"I like this type of terrain better than that awful gor ...," the eight-year-old was saying.

"What's that white thing over there?" the six-year-old interrupted.

"You mean the roundish thing? Don't know. Let's take a look!"

Tromping off into the sparse vegetation, they quickly located the object. It was a human skull. It appeared to have lain there for years, baking in the sun. There were bits of dried flesh stuck to it. A clump of hair, bleached by the sun to a light reddish-brown, was attached to the crown.

"*AÑAU!*" the boys exclaimed in unison.

Excited by their find, they were soon searching for the rest of the skeleton. K'uchi-Wara picked up some leg and foot bones, ribs, a shoulder blade, then a pelvis. For his part, Qispi discovered arm bones, another skull, vertebrae, a pelvis, and hand bones. Each new acquisition was punctuated by a whoop or holler! As it turned out, the entire field was strewn with skeletal parts. Many of them were still linked by tough ligaments. When the older child examined one piece closely, he found that it was not really white. Rather it was a light yellow. *It feels greasy. And there are gnaw marks all over it, probably made by rats and mice.*

"HEY! BOYS! Get over here, *posthaste!* What do you think you're doing?" It was the Old One.

While the children had been busy searching for bones, the rest of the party, who had been walking at a slower pace, caught up to them.

"Look what we found," Qispi said proudly. He marched up to the priest and presented him with a human jawbone. "Lots and lots of dead people."

"So I see!" responded the Old One gruffly. "But it's not appropriate for sacred *qhapaq huchas* to defile themselves. You're handling the foul remains of rebels."

"What do you mean?" asked K'uchi-Wara. "Who were these people? There must be hundreds of skeletons."

"Probably *thousands!*" said the Inka official, who had joined the group. "They were a provincial people who swore allegiance to King Thupa Yapanqui. But then they betrayed him by revolting. As was his right and duty, he returned with an army and decimated them. He ordered that their bodies be left unburied. That way, the pumas and vultures and foxes could feed on them."

"*Thus always to traitors!*" said the Old One, as he spat on the ground.

K'uchi-Wara's parents met up with the rest of the party. "You see?" his father whispered into his mother's ear in Aymara. "That's what would've happened to us if we'd not let our son become a *qhapaq hucha!*"

* * *

While traveling on the royal highway, when the shadows began to lengthen and they decided it was time to stop for the night, the state official would find a *chaski*. The *chaskis* were runners who carried messages. They operated as part of a relay system, and were stationed in huts every tenth of a *tupu* (every half mile). The official would send the runner to the next *tampu* with the news that they would be arriving. By the time they reached the lodging house, its caretakers would be preparing their dinner and beds. K'uchi-Wara always enjoyed his stays at the *tampus*.

It was late evening, and the family had retired to their room. The lodging-house where they were spending the night was located outside a hamlet, among the rolling hills. K'uchi-Wara sat on his sleeping platform, staring pensively out the window. He watched a sparrow. It tried to keep its balance while perched on a tall stem that arched under its weight and moved in the breeze. The stem was part of a sea of swaying bunchgrasses whose color changed from gold to pink to red as the sun set. When the color completely drained from the scene outside, the boy turned his attention to what was happening inside. His parents were cuddling.

What would it be like to hold a girl? I wish I'd tried it with Nina before I left home. She's adventuresome, always eager to try new things. So I bet that she'd have been willing. First I'd have reached over and stroked her hair. Then, after looking into her dark brown eyes, I'd have gently brushed her cheek with the tips of my fingers. Next I'd have wrapped my arms around her and held her close for a long time. How would her body feel against mine? Soft and warm? Would I have felt the beating of her heart? I'll never know, though, because I didn't take the chance. Now it's too late.

On another occasion, dusty and tired after a long day on the road, the group arrived at a *tampu* in the middle of a Collagua village. *I like this village,* K'uchi-Wara thought. *A lot of the places where we've stayed have been run-down and poor. This one's well-kept and pretty.* The buildings were made of fieldstones set in a mortar of mud. They were plastered inside and out. But whereas the lodging house, as an Inka structure, was rectangular, the Collagua dwellings were round. The thatched roofs of their houses were cone-shaped with steep pitches and pointy tops.

Outside the *tampu* was an old man. K'uchi-Wara took a look at him, and immediately did a double-take. His cranium had the same outline as the roofs. It was tall and tapered to a point. The eight-year-old touched Qispi lightly on the shoulder to get his attention. Then, with a flick of his head in the direction of the elder, he whispered in his friend's ear.

"Look at that guy. He's deformed."

"*Atatau!* How horrible!"

Imagine the boys' surprise when they entered the Inka *tampu* and met the caretakers, who also had cone-shaped crowns.

Does everyone in this village have a deformed head? K'uchi-Wara wondered. *What's this all about?* He was too polite and self-conscious, however, to ask his hosts about their craniums. And he didn't get a chance to question his parents, at least not that night.

At sunrise, the party continued on their way. It was a beautiful day. To the east, the bright light reflected off the eternal snows of the high peaks. K'uchi-Wara walked with his father. "Dad?"

"Yes."

"Why do the people here have such strange heads?"

His father laughed. "You know, I had the same question. I asked about it."

"And?"

"It turns out that the Collagua bind the heads of their babies to give them a cone-shape."

"But *why?*" The child had endless curiosity, which sometimes drove his parents crazy.

"See the mountain over there?" His father indicated a high volcano crowned with white.

"Sure."

"That's Collaguata. The Collagua worship it as their major *waqa*. They honor it by reproducing its form in their children's heads."

"*Wat'ax*—that's pretty *odd!*"

"I've heard there's another group that's native to this province. They're called the Cavana. They consider a peak called Gualca-gualca to be sacred. Gualca-gualca has a big broad summit. They venerate their *waqa* by tying a board to the foreheads of their newborns, which makes their skulls wide and flat."

"I repeat—that's pretty *odd!*"

"I suppose so. But keep in mind that some of our practices, which are perfectly normal to us, would seem strange to them."

* * *

The three llama train drivers, after consulting with the Inka official, decided it was time for the party to leave the royal highway. They knew from personal experience that the road would be meandering far to the west. As they wanted to keep the route as straight as possible, they struck out across the open terrain.

Once again, K'uchi-Wara was walking alongside an animal-driver. He said, "I've been trying to figure out how you guide us when we go cross-country. I have to admit, I don't see how you do it."

The man smiled. "It's simple."

"Maybe for you!"

"Okay, here's how. I've made this trip before. And I've memorized many features of the landscape—features that *really* stand out. They include mountains, strange rock formations, and cliff faces. These landmarks are strung along our route like the beads on a necklace. Do you understand?"

K'uchi-Wara nodded.

"When one of my landmarks comes into view, I head straight for it. I try to keep it in my sight. By the time our group reaches it, there's always another mountain or other feature on the horizon. And I head for it. By following a series of sight lines toward the landmarks, I can get us across the open spaces. Safely and surely. Make sense?"

K'uchi-Wara nodded again.

* * *

The drivers led the party cross-country. They were on a lofty plain that reminded Qispi of the ocean on a calm day: both were vast, with gentle swells. The bunchgrasses that grew here were sparse, and barely reached the six-year-old's knees. As they walked, they steadily climbed. The child could see that they were slowly making their way toward some high volcanoes that were lined up like sentinels standing at attention. The Old One pointed at each peak and named it for the boy. "There's Ampato and Chachani and Pichu-Pichu and Putina. They're all very sacred. And all of them have received offerings of *qhapaq huchas*."

The group had to traverse an occasional arroyo, which slowed their progress. Although Qispi didn't know it, the arroyos had their origins among the volcanoes: water from melting snow and ice formed braided rivulets that descended from the heights. The rivulets came together as gushing streams, which themselves joined to become swift rivers. The rivers cut deep gashes in the earth, exposing walls of tuff. As the party made their way into one of the arroyos, the six-year-old could see layer upon layer of the soft white stone, built up from one volcanic eruption after another.

While traveling across the open country, when the sun neared the horizon the animal drivers would look for a good place to camp. They always chose level spots with running water nearby. They would unload the gear from the backs of the llamas, after which the attendants would erect the tents. The attendants first set up a framework of poles, over which they stretched llama skins that had been stitched together. The tents were anchored with rocks, if any could be found, and if not, with wooden pegs. Then they would lay out the beds. The bedding consisted of bundles of grass woven together to form mattresses, along with woolen blankets.

Lastly the attendants would build a fire using wood brought by the llamas, over which they would cook dinner. Dinner was usually a soup or stew prepared with different combinations of dried corn, *quinua, chuño*, and *ch'arkhi*. The dishes were flavored with hot chili peppers and herbs. After trying a particularly spicy dish, the two boys were heard to exclaim, "*Jaw, jaw!*" Neither Qispi, nor K'uchi-Wara, nor their parents had to help with any of the camp chores.

The closer the group got to the volcanoes, the greater the altitude and the lower the temperature. One day when they emerged from their snug tents, they discovered the earth covered in white. It had snowed during the night. It was still snowing.

The Inka official told the others, "Visibility's poor. It would make sense to spend the day here. By tomorrow the storm should be over, and we can continue on our way." The rest of the party agreed.

Qispi and K'uchi-Wara were standing outside, delighting in the white world. The six-year-old said, "*Alalau*–how cold! But how *amazing!*" He had borrowed the latter word from K'uchi-Wara's vocabulary. He felt the nearly imperceptible weight of flakes as they fluttered onto the ends of his lashes. Some lit on the tip of his nose, which tickled. He giggled and gave his nose an itch. Then he stuck out his tongue to catch more flakes, which melted the instant they landed. "You know, this is the first time I've seen snow close-up. On the north coast, it never snows."

"Is that so," replied the older boy, a slight smile crossing his lips. He knelt and scooped up a pile of the white stuff with his bare hands. "Then you don't know what snow's good for, do you?" He packed the fluffy mass into a nice round ball.

"What do you mean?" asked the younger child, suddenly suspicious.

"Oh, nothing," said K'uchi-Wara, all innocence. Just then he jumped up, drew his arm back, and hurled the snowball. SMACK. He hit the six-year-old squarely in the chest. For a second, Qispi was too stunned to react. A dark and determined look crossed his face. The next instant, he was down on the ground, making his own snowballs. What followed was an epic battle. When it was over, the boys were wet, cold, and exhausted. They were happy too.

The next day, the group resumed their travels. Trudging through a sea of white, the going was taxing. Qispi was in such a good mood, however, *nothing* could spoil it. *The snow's not so deep. And I can turn our hike into a game. I can try stepping into each of K'uchi-Wara's footprints. It might be hard to do, though, 'cause his legs are longer than mine.* The sky was overcast, and a wind was blowing. *But it's at my back, so it just pushes me along.* As the wind picked up, it began to pelt the child's neck and head with spindrift. Not even *that* seemed to bother him, though. Looking up from the tracks he followed, he was thrilled to see the ice crystals give form to the moving air. *The snow's dancing!* Indeed, the spindrift took the shape of a curtain that billowed in the currents for several seconds before breaking up. Then the ice crystals reassembled into a pattern of interconnected curlicues, which coalesced into a tight little funnel that swirled around and around before dissolving.

* * *

The Old One's reaction to the snow was completely different from Qispi's. *This is a sign from the mountain-gods! They're demanding an offering from us. If we don't deliver, they'll bar our way south.*

It was evening when they stopped at the foot of Putina's massive cinder-cone. The Old One ordered the attendants and llama drivers to seize a llama with white wool. "Hold it tightly with its head facing the mountain," he told them. Then he commanded K'uchi-Wara and Qispi to kneel before him. As the sun's disk touched the western horizon, the peak's white slopes were set ablaze with color. The priest grabbed a knife, pulled the animal's head back to expose its throat, and slit its jugular. Blood spurted out. He collected some of it in a ceramic bowl. When the heart had beat its last and the hot liquid had stopped flowing, he dipped his fingers into the bowl. He sprinkled blood toward Ampato, Chachani, and Pichu-Pichu, while invoking the mountain spirits. Then the Old One sent Waman to fetch a small dried gourd, whose outside was decorated with a geometric pattern, and his sling. After filling the gourd with red liquid, he hurled it with his sling as far up Putina's slope as possible. There it smashed to pieces. Its contents, an offering, spattered all over. The priest used the remaining blood to draw a line across each *qhapaq hucha*'s face, from ear to ear, and passing over the bridge of his nose.

He prayed, "Oh, *waqas*, our beloved ancestors, accept the sacrifice that I make to you! In return, show us, your descendants, compassion. Give us fair weather, keep us safe during our journey. Grant that we may reach our destination without mishap. I beseech you in the name of the Inka, our sovereign lord."

* * *

K'uchi-Wara spent the night tossing and turning. He had a nightmare too. In it he was approached by a parade of a dozen *qhapaq huchas* who had been sacrificed to the volcano gods. Most of them were girls and young women, although there were a few boys too. They wore fine clothing and elegant adornments. From a distance, they appeared to have comely faces. They cheerfully called to him, saying, "Come, K'uchi-Wara, come away with us. You can live with us in the house of the gods. We'll have fun together. You'll see!" Intrigued by their words and captivated by their melodious voices, K'uchi-Wara went toward them.

As he did so, however, he saw that their cheeks were sunken, their eyes black hollows. Their smiles were the frozen grimaces of *rigor mortis*. Moving closer still, he was shocked to find that each bore the mark of his or her specific form of sacrifice. A girl strangled with a cord had a scarlet groove circling her neck. A young woman dispatched with a club had a swollen head. A boy whose throat had been cut had a gaping wound. No blood was left in it. K'uchi-Wara wanted to turn away from the *qhapaq huchas* and run. His legs wouldn't carry him, though. Finally he stood face to face with the boy, who was his age. Against his will, he looked into the child's dark eyes. They seemed to suck him into them and to hold him fast. He struggled in a growing pool of blackness. He was drowning in a sea of pitch. Suddenly he found himself alone on a mountain-top. It was drenched in sunlight. The wind was whipping spindrift around with great force, and he could feel the sharp sting of the ice crystals against his skin. "MAMA!" he called out. "Mama ... where are you? Mama?"

"Wake up, K'uchi-Wara," he heard his mother say. "Wake up. You're having a bad dream. It's okay now. I'm here."

The child opened his eyes. He was in a tent, the sides of which were flapping in the wind. He was with his parents. Apparently he had yelled something in his sleep because both of them were wide awake and staring at him.

"Are you all right?" his father asked.

He was not. The terror of the nightmare was fresh in his mind and he started to cry. He sobbed uncontrollably. Although his mother tried cradling him in her arms and speaking comforting words to him, he was inconsolable.

Their journey continued in the morning.

Early in the morning, the llama-drivers pack an animal for the trip
ahead

Chapter Ten: The Incredible Journey

As the group made their way south, they cut across deep valleys that extended from the mountains in the east to the ocean in the west. Up, up, up they would go to the crest of a high ridge. Then down, down, down to the floor of the valley below, after which it would be up, up, up again to the top of the next ridge.

K'uchi-Wara was five weeks into his journey and had already taken well over a million steps. He gazed at the steep slope that rose on the far side of the valley—yet another valley to be traversed! He could make out a thin line, the royal highway, which ascended in a series of long switchbacks. Near the top, though, where the highway met a vertical rock-band, it just vanished.

That's strange! It reminds me of the horrible gorge, where the road also disappeared. He dropped back to where the Inka official was walking. Sidling up to him, the boy said, "Sir, you've been on this road before, haven't you?"

"Yes, many times."

"What happens to it when it reaches the top of that rise?" K'uchi-Wara indicated the far slope. "It seems to disappear."

"Very observant of you. But I'm not going to tell you where the road goes! You'll just have to see for *yourself*." The man smiled.

"That's not very helpful,"the child muttered under his breath.

K'uchi-Wara and Qispi, who had begun walking together, reached the foot of the slope and started up. As the eight-year-old had seen from afar, it was very steep, so the highway ascended in zigzags. Walking back and forth, back and forth, they slowly made their way skyward. The sun was hot, the humidity high, and the climbing taxing. After what felt like an eternity, the boys plopped down. Beads of sweat rolled down K'uchi-Wara's brown face, some of which got into his eyes, stinging them. He panted, "This ... humidity ... is awful! ... Look at me ... I'm sweating like ... like I have a fever.... Where I come from, the air's always dry."

"Are ... you *kidding*?" Qispi gasped. "This ... is *nothing*.... At home on the coast ... sometimes it gets so ... so humid that ... that you feel like you're swimming!"

"That sounds terrible. How do you survive?"

"You get used to it."

After a rest, they continued up the switchbacks: back and forth, back and forth.

As the day wore on, the slope became increasingly rocky. The road wound around large boulders that seemed delicately balanced on the incline. It made its way up and over outcrops of bedrock. K'uchi-Wara, having left Qispi way behind, could see it was approaching a rock wall that was at least fifty feet high. He was curious to know what the road did when it reached the wall, but also anxious about the possibility of having to scale the wall. He was a short distance behind the Old One, who walked around an enormous slab of stone ... and vanished. The boy followed. Rounding the rock, he found himself alone at the foot of the wall. *Where's the Old One gone?* Then he noticed the entrance to a tunnel. It was invisible to people in the valley and to those climbing the slope, being hidden behind the slab. K'uchi-Wara peered into it. *It's a huge crack in the rock that the Inkas have made even bigger, so that a man can stand up. And look, they've carved steps too.* The steep steps led up into the gloom. As the eight-year-old mounted them, it got darker and darker. Finally he had to put his hands against the wall of the tunnel to feel his way. He heard voices echoing behind him. When he turned around, though, he could see nothing. Whoever was below was blocking the tiny patch of light from the entrance. *"Way!"* he whispered into the blackness, and gave a slight shudder. He went on.

Suddenly a blinding radiance appeared. It grew in size as he approached it. *The other entrance!* Before reaching it, the child caught a glimpse of the Old One, his distinct and unsmiling profile silhouetted against the white light. Then the boy burst out of the tunnel, glad to be in the open air again. He was at the top of the ridge, above the rock wall.

Making their way across the floor of another valley, the party came to a deep chasm. At the bottom of it was a raging river. As the source of the river was a glacier, its waters were greenish-blue in color and *cold.* Racing along in its course, it formed a series of rapids. The churning current surged over and around boulders, creating large stationary waves, and shooting white spray and foam in all directions. Even from where they stood high above the water, the boys heard the ROAR of the rapids.

"How're we going to cross?" Qispi asked, a note of dread in his voice.

K'uchi-Wara pointed upstream. A slender swinging-bridge connected their side of the gorge to the opposite one.

"What? Are you *crazy?* We're going to cross on *that* thing?"

From a distance, the bridge, though elegant looking with its U-shape, did not inspire much confidence. Spanning the vast expanse, it seemed to be little more than a thread that would snap in the slightest breeze.

They walked along the cliff's edge to the bridge. Approaching it, K'uchi-Wara realized that it was more substantial than he had thought. On each side of the gorge, the Inkas had erected a pair of massive stone pillars. Between the pillars they had set large wooden beams. Tied to these horizontal beams and stretching over the raging river were five cables, three of which comprised the floor. The remaining two served as handrails. To complete the bridge, the Inkas had attached wooden slats to the floor cables.

When I use this bridge, K'uchi-Wara said to himself, *my life will depend on the strength of the cables.* So he carefully inspected them. They had been artfully crafted, and represented a considerable amount of time and effort. The Inkas had twisted dried *ichu* grass to make twine, had braided the twine to produce cordage, had combined the cords to create rope, and had plaited the ropes to make cables. Each cable was six inches in diameter.

The official called his charges together. "If I can have your attention! We're going to cross the *q'iswa chaka*. Though it might look precarious, I assure you that traversing it is perfectly safe. Safe, that is, if we follow some simple rules. We'll go one at a time. The *qhapaq huchas*, who are the most important members of the group, will go last. As you cross, keep your hands on the guard-rails. And look straight ahead. Never look down! It'll make you dizzy. Also, do not—I repeat, do not—walk with even steps! Take some short ones, some long ones, then more short ones."

"Why?" K'uchi-Wara asked, his curiosity getting the better of him.

"Because if you walk rhythmically, the cables will start bobbing up and down in unison, following the rhythm of your gait. The bobbing will become more and more pronounced. It may become so extreme that it bounces you right off the bridge! So remember to vary your steps. Is that understood?"

Everyone nodded.

"Okay, *I'll* go first. Watch how *I* do it. Follow *my* lead."

The man clambered up onto the structure. He put his hands on the side cables, fixed his gaze on something in the distance, and started walking. He varied his gait as he went. The closer he got to the middle of the bridge, the more it sagged under his weight. He did not falter, though. The wind picked up and the slender structure started swaying. Still he continued. After a while, he reached the far side of the chasm. He waved his arms to indicate that the next person should cross.

Before the Old One began his traverse, he faced the sun and said a little prayer. "Oh, Inti, lord of the heavens, preserve me from harm." He plucked an eyebrow and blew it into the air. He was followed by Waman, by K'uchi-Wara's parents, by Qispi's parents, and by the attendants. As the llama train drivers and their animals could not cross the bridge, they had headed downstream. At a spot where the river widened and the current slowed, they could safely ford.

It was K'uchi-Wara's turn to cross. Both he and Qispi had been waiting for several "hours." To the former boy, who had often watched his mother cook, an "hour" was the time required to boil a pot of potatoes on the stove. Of course, they had put the hours to good use. They had discussed in graphic detail everything that could possibly go wrong! Thus when he finally climbed up onto the structure, the eight-year-old had the horrible feeling that he was mounting the scaffolding to his own execution. He put his small hands on the guard rails. He stared into the distance. Across the chasm, he saw tiny figures gesturing him forward. He took a deep breath. Shivering with excitement and terror-stricken at the same time, he took the first tentative step ... and another ... and another. "Hey, this isn't so *bad!*" He took some more steps. Reaching the center of the span, it seemed as if he were surrounded by a boundless gulf. He yelled as loudly as he could, "*WAQE!* I'M A CONDOR! I CAN DO THIS!" He was as good as his word, for he got across without any problems.

* * *

The same cannot be said of Qispi. Once his friend had made it safely to the other side, he felt alone and scared. His hands trembled as he dragged himself onto the bridge. His head swirled with visions of disaster as he started crossing. In his haste to traverse quickly so that he could rejoin the party, he forgot everything the Inka official had told them. His gait became mechanical. He took steps that were automatic and rhythmic as if he were marching, because that was the only way he could make himself walk. But his movements created harmonic waves in the structure. It began to bounce UP-AND-DOWN, UP-AND-DOWN, UP-AND-DOWN! Qispi stopped. He held onto the handrail for dear life. His breathing was quick and shallow. After a while, however, the bobbing subsided. He heaved a sigh of relief. When he started walking again, he made sure it was with uneven steps.

This was *not* the six-year-old's day. He had made it past the mid-point of the span, the bottom of the "U," and was working his way up the far side. He could see his parents waving to him, urging him on. Then the wind began to blow, the structure to sway. BACK-AND-FORTH, **BACK-AND-FORTH, BACK-AND-FORTH.** He grabbed one of the side cables and made the worst possible mistake: he looked down. Faaaaaaaar below was the swirling, churning water of the rapids. He felt dizzy! He wanted to vomit. And he completely froze. He could move neither forward, nor backward.

* * *

From their side of the gorge, Qispi's parents watched the unfolding scene with growing alarm. When his mother saw him desperately cling-ing to the swinging bridge, she became frantic. "Somebody *do* some-thing! *Save my son!*"

K'uchi-Wara knew *exactly* what had to be done. Waiting for a lull in the wind, he bounded onto the bridge and quickly made his way to the terror-stricken boy. He was careful not to start the structure bobbing again.

Reaching Qispi, he looked him in the eye and tried to reassure him. "It's okay. You're going to be fine. The wind's died down, the bridge has stopped swaying. I want you to walk with me to the other side. Think you can do that?"

The six-year-old nodded.

"Good! We're going to go slow. No need to rush. As we walk, we're going to look straight ahead. And we're *not* going to move in unison. Do you understand?"

Qispi nodded.

Shortly thereafter, the boys arrived safe and sound at the edge of the chasm. While Qispi's mother and father were hugging their son, Waman was hailing K'uchi-Wara as a hero. Patting the child on the back, he said, "You're very *brave!*"

* * *

The Old One barked, "Waman, I want a word with you." As the two men walked away from the rest of the group, the senior priest said, "Courageous? You think K'uchi-Wara was being courageous back there?"

"Of course! What would *you* call him?"

"*Foolish*, that's what! Both *qhapaq huchas* could have perished, which would've been catastrophic!"

"But they didn't, thanks to K'uchi-Wara."

"Look," said the Old One, "I've seen this type of behavior before. In other *qhapaq huchas*. It's especially prevalent in boys. They take great risks in order to confront their own mortality."

"What? Are you saying the boy saved his friend as a way of coping with his fear? Fear over his upcoming sacrifice?"

"That's *exactly* what I'm saying! Hence I want you to keep an eye on K'uchi-Wara. Make sure he doesn't attempt any more heroics. Is that understood?"

* * *

Day after day, the group continued their seemingly endless march south. K'uchi-Wara measured their progress by watching the succession of mountains toward the east. The peaks had distinct shapes. They ranged from tall spires to rounded domes to broad flat tops to enormous fangs to perfect cones to sawtooth ridges.

The boy was fascinated to see how the appearance of a summit changed as the light changed. On a bright hazy day, the image of a mountain might be flat, distant, indistinct, and devoid of hue. In the evening, when the light softened and acquired a golden tone, a peak could become fully three-dimensional. It might appear to be so close that you could reach out and touch it. Its colors would be vibrant.

At night, the form of a mountain might be reduced to a sharp-edged profile: the line where the luminescence of the Milky Way met the blackness of the mountain's bulk. If there was a full moon, the ice and snow on the flanks of a peak might glow with a silvery shine so bright you could read a *khipu* by it.

K'uchi-Wara also was struck by the different types of clouds and by their relationship with the summits. Sometimes a cloud resembled a lacy grey veil drawn across the face of a peak. At other times, it was more like a piece of cotton shredded by the black spike of a mountaintop. *Oh, look at that cloud. Its long shape reminds me of a sleeping giant. He's resting his head on the rolling hill, which is his headrest.*

* * *

Zapahuira was an administrative center in the highlands of northern Chile. The weary travelers arrived there late one afternoon. They stayed for several days, resting for the next leg of their journey. They were housed in a large compound consisting of a suite of rooms arranged around a central patio and surrounded by a perimeter wall. The structure was made of fieldstones held together with mortar. Its roof was thatched.

K'uchi-Wara got a good night's sleep. Then, being the restless type, who was always eager to try new things, he met up with Qispi. "Let's go exploring," he told the younger boy. And so they did. Near the lodging house, they discovered a set of terraces that the Inkas had built on the side of a steep hill. A gang of men with wooden hoes was spread out over the terraces, working diligently. Whereas K'uchi-Wara tended to be more reserved when alone, with Qispi he often felt emboldened. To impress his friend, he marched up to the nearest laborer and started talking to him.

"Hi. Qispi and I are visiting your town. We were wondering what you're doing?"

The man smiled, partly because he was amused by the boy's directness and partly because he saw an opportunity to take a break. He leaned against his long-handled hoe and gave the children an enthusiastic, "*Napaykullayki*—hello! We're just weedin' the terraces."

Although the man spoke Quechua, his pronunciation was such that K'uchi-Wara had trouble understanding him. He replied, "Are you working for your *kuraka*?"

Before answering, the man reached into the cloth bag at his waist and pulled out several coca leaves. He popped them into his mouth along with a bit of crushed lime. As he chewed, he said, "No, we're raisin' potatoes for the Inkas. It's part of our *mit'a* obligations. You know what that is, don't you?"

K'uchi-Wara shook his head.

"It's a tax, see. You pay by workin' a set number of days each year. We farm. Others serve in the army, or herd state-owned llamas, or man fortresses, or build roads, or ..."

"Do some people go to Cuzco as guestworkers? To help build walls?" the boy interrupted.

"I guess so."

"That's what our guide in the capital told us." K'uchi-Wara scanned the slope, eyeing the terraces. They appeared to have been planted in the same crop. "What do you do with so many potatoes?"

"That's a good question. After we harvest them, we lay them out in the air to dry. Then we put them in storehouses. They'll keep for ages. Should the harvest fail, on account of drought or blight, we can survive by eatin' them. Also, llama trains haul loads of them to the coast. The fisher-folk on the coast don't raise potatoes. They send us dried fish in return ..."

"Oh," interjected the boy excitedly, "we have a trading system like that in my homeland!"

"Okay," said the man. "Well, the coastal people send us *guano* too. Llama trains full of it!"

"What's *guano*?"

"What's *guano*, you ask! Don't you know? I thought that *everyone* in the world knew about *guano*!" These taunts came from Qispi.

"Well, maybe everyone on the *coast* knows what it is. But I'm not *from* the coast, am I!"

"If you *really* want to know–it's BIRD SHIT!"

"Bird shit? What's it good for?"

"It's a fertilizer. If you mix it into your soil, see, you'll get a better crop," answered the man.

"So, who are you boys? I haven't seen you before. You said you were in Cuzco, and that you're visitin' here. Where you goin'?"

Qispi stepped forward and proudly announced, "We're *qhapaq huchas*! We're on our way south. We're going to take part in some sacred rites. We're staying in the *tampu* over there."

The blood drained from the laborer's face. He dropped to his knees, averting his eyes. He blubbered, "As the Sun's my witness, I ... I ... had no idea you're *qhapaq huchas*! Forgive me! If I'd known, I'd never have acted so familiar. Please don't tell the Inkas! If they found out I talked to you, I'd be in *real* trouble!"

K'uchi-Wara and Qispi were confused and embarrassed by the man's reaction to them. They promised to keep what had happened a secret. The laborer went back to weeding the terraces. He did not say another word to them, nor did he look at them as they turned and headed back to the lodging house.

The Inka road led the boys and their party from Zapahuira to Lake Chungará. From the moment he laid eyes on this body of water, K'uchi-Wara was stunned by its beauty. It was the color of lapis lazuli. Stately black-and-white geese drifted across it, while a flock of flamingoes waded in its shallows. Some of the pink birds were feeding, dragging their large bills through the water upside down. Others were vocalizing. They made all kinds of sounds, from grunts to squawks to honks. Among the plants dotting the shore, mostly bunchgrasses and dark green cushion plants, wandered a flock of Andean ostriches. The boy also was impressed by the Payachatas or "twins." This pair of ice-clad volcanoes towered over the lake. One of them had a perfectly symmetrical cone.

While the child gawked at the sacred peaks, the priests honored them. The men faced the *waqas* and bowed in a show of humility. They stretched their arms out in front of themselves so that the limbs were parallel and somewhat higher than their heads. Then they opened their hands with the palms toward the volcanoes. Making a kissing sound with their mouths, they brought their hands to their lips and kissed their finger-tips. The rite ended with a prayer. "Oh, mountain-gods, preserve the lord Inka. Give him peace and prosperity!"

From Lake Chungará, the travelers continued south to the Atacama Desert. They followed the royal highway, which had been placed along the western slope of the Andes. The road was two and a half paces wide. It was marked on either side by stone cairns, and had been made by removing rocks from its path. Along with it, the Inkas had built a string of *tampus*. They were always located next to springs or along streams that descended from the heights, so water would be available to travelers.

It was early in the morning when the Inka official called a meeting. The group had spent the previous night in one of the roadside inns. They were getting ready to leave.

"*Paxtan*—a word of warning to all of you! We'll soon be entering the Atacama Desert. This is the driest and roughest part of the realm. And it's the major obstacle to our reaching our destination. I don't want to alarm you, especially not the *qhapaq huchas*. But we've lost people while crossing the desert. In most cases, the people died of dehydration."

"What does that mean?" K'uchi-Wara asked.

"What? 'Dehydration'? It means they lost too much water from their bodies. So while you're walking, be sure to drink plenty of fluids! Also, try to cover up as much as possible. If at any time you start to feel dizzy or nauseous, or if you become exhausted or get muscle cramps, I want you to stop. Sit down and rest. And as I say, replenish your fluids."

As they journeyed into the Atacama, what little vegetation there had been all but disappeared. And what sparse population there had been, likewise vanished. They entered an unbelievably desolate world. They trekked through rock-strewn valleys resembling features on the moon. They climbed up jagged ridges baking under a cruel sun. They trudged over huge sand dunes slowly moving under the constant pressure of a hot wind.

As is often the case in the Atacama, the sun was unbearably bright, the heat oppressive. The group was following the highway as it skirted a chain of low hills. These hills were rocky and barren. K'uchi-Wara and Qispi were walking alongside one of the llama drivers, when the eight-year-old stopped. "Phew." He wiped the sweat from his forehead and scanned their surroundings. Suddenly he let out a loud "*AÑAU.*" Pointing at the slope above, he exclaimed, "Look! There's a giant llama—and another, and another. It's a whole caravan of monster animals."

Qispi chimed in, "Oh, do you see? They're being led by two huge llama drivers."

"Who made this giant picture?" K'uchi-Wara asked the llama driver. "Why did they do it in the middle of no ..."

"And *how* did they do it?" Qispi interrupted.

"Hold on, hold on," the driver said, laughing and raising both hands to call for silence. "You *two* are some of the most curious kids I've ever met. To begin with, this particular landscape drawing was made years ago. By some caravan drivers. It's meant to tell travelers like us that we're on the right road. Ahead you'll see lots more pictures. They were created by the different groups who live around the desert. Many have religious meaning.

"Now, to answer your question, Qispi. Look closely at one of the llamas." He directed their attention to the hillside. "If you squint, you can see that the outline of the figure was made by piling up stones. Then the darker sunburnt soil inside the figure was removed. And the lighter soil underneath was exposed."

"I get it," said K'uchi-Wara.

"So do *I*," echoed Qispi, though he seemed confused.

Walking along the road together, the boys kept an eye out for more landscape-drawings. They saw geometric designs, all kinds of animals, and human figures. Coming around a bend, Qispi pointed out the representation of a buck. "Look at that llama! He's got a *big* penis. What's he doing to that other llama?"

"I think they're mating. Haven't you seen animals mating?"

"You forget. We don't have llamas and alpacas where I live."

"Oh, right." K'uchi-Wara's mind drifted to his own homeland. During his life, he had often watched bucks mounting female alpacas. As he had lived with his parents in a small one-room house, he had even heard them discreetly having sex. *It's no big deal. I wonder what it feels like, though. If I hadn't left Wila-Nayra, would I have gotten together with Nina? Would we have mated and had children?*

In the afternoon, they passed a solitary hill with a long gentle slope. Extending up the slope was the largest and strangest landscape-drawing they had seen so far. It was the stick-figure of a man. Turning to Qispi, K'uchi-Wara said, "You took part in the *qhapaq hucha* festival in Cuzco, didn't you?"

"Yeah, why?"

"Well, did you see the statue of Inti? You know, he's the Sun God."

"I guess I saw it, but don't remember so well. Cuzco's mostly a blur to me. I was pretty scared while I was there."

"That's too bad," said K'uchi-Wara, sympathetic to his friend. "As I recall, Inti's statue has solar rays shooting out of its head. So does this guy. The statue also has pumas between its legs. And look, this guy's got a puma on each side of his waist. So maybe *this* is the local people's idea of the Sun God."

Several days later, they were walking in the shadow of a mountain, when they passed a lake. *That's strange! Its water's white. Not clear, but white.* Nearby they came to another lake, whose water was a bright turquoise. K'uchi-Wara was thirsty. Thinking to himself, *I don't want to die of de-hy-dra-tion*, he dropped down the bank to the shore of the lake. He cupped his hands and dipped them into the water. It was cold. He brought his hands to his lips and drank, but quickly spat out the liquid. *It tastes terrible!*

The royal highway skirted a field of fumaroles. Some of them were spewing steam, while others were belching clouds of gas that smelled like rotten duck eggs. Many of the fumaroles had yellow rings around them. The party had just passed them by, holding their noses, when they heard a loud WHOOSH coming from the left. Turning, they saw a fountain of boiling water starting to erupt from a vent in the earth. As the water shot higher and higher, it gave rise to great billows of steam. After a brief period, the geyser had spent its force and the column of water died down.

On another occasion, K'uchi-Wara stopped to pee. As he was fond of doing, he aimed the stream at an object, in this case a large black rock. He was alarmed to see the liquid evaporate as soon as it spattered on the rock. He gazed out over the vast plain that remained to be crossed, heat-waves rising from it. *What have we gotten ourselves into? Will we really be able to make it across this desert?*

Qispi and his parents set eyes on Mount Aconcagua for the first time

Chapter Eleven: The Journey Continues

Twelve weeks into the journey, the boy having taken two and three-quarters of a million steps, he and his entourage arrived at Catarpe. This settlement and administrative center lies in the heart of the Atacama Desert. The official had been to the settlement before. He made no secret of the fact that he was proud of the Inka state, and that he thought the "provincials" in his charge should be impressed by it too. Hence he offered to show K'uchi-Wara's parents around the place. The mother declined. As she never tired of telling her husband, "I despise the Inkas! I want as little to do with them as possible. And I don't think you should be so eager to associate with them."

The father was caught in a bind. *I have no love for them either. But I can't afford to alienate them. They're going to make me the lord of all the lands around Wila-Nayra, so I have to work with them. I suppose one could accuse me of collaborating with the enemy. Then again, what choice do I have? It's either cooperate or die. The Inkas would not hesitate to kill me, my family, and the rest of Wila-Nayra's residents, just like they massacred the thousands of people in the field that we passed.* He reluctantly accepted the offer.

Catarpe, which was situated on a flat-top mesa, was typical of imperial settlements. It was laid out on a grid plan. As the two men strolled down the straight lanes between rectangular buildings, the official explained, "Our primary interest in the region is mining. Although there's some gold and silver here, we mostly extract copper and semi-precious stones. The locals have a long history of exploiting mineral resources. They're very skilled at it. So after we subjugated them, we put them to work in the mines."

The father nodded. *How much longer do I have to put up with this?* Despite his lack of enthusiasm, questions occurred to him that he genuinely wanted answered. "We're in the middle of the harshest desert in the empire, right?"

"Right."

"So where do the people get their water? And their food, for that matter? How can the state maintain such a large settlement in such a dry place?"

"To answer your first question, we're in an oasis. It's sustained by lots of springs. Without them, nothing would survive. To answer your second question, my people have built many agricultural terraces, irrigation canals, and storehouses in the area. We've also assigned part of the populace to raise crops. Believe it or not, we produce enough food to feed everyone here. And there's enough surplus to provision all the *tampus* in the region, even the more remote ones."

They walked to a plaza in the center of the settlement. It was delineated by a low wall. From there they could see a line of snow-capped volcanoes toward the east. Achalau—*how beautiful!* the father thought, despite his determination to take no pleasure in the tour.

*   *   *

Meanwhile the boys amused themselves as best they could. The Old One had prohibited them from having any contact with the local children, whom he said would "pollute" them.

"Sometimes I hate being a *qhapaq hucha*," complained K'uchi-Wara. "Why shouldn't we have fun with other kids?"

"Yeah," Qispi agreed. "But at least we have each other to play with." Ever since K'uchi-Wara had rescued him on the bridge, he had looked up to the older boy and had felt a growing affection for him. "You *promised* to show me how to use a sling. How about now?"

"Okay."

No self-respecting Lupaka male would ever have admitted to not knowing how to use a sling. Such was not the case with the Moche, however, whose weapon of choice was a wooden sword. K'uchi-Wara sprinted to the building where they were staying. He returned a short time later with a braided cord in his hand. Although it had been a long while since he had wielded the weapon, he was *not* going to miss an opportunity to show off with it. The boys made a target by stacking large stones. Then, standing a good distance from it, the eight-year-old picked up a rock, which he fitted to the pouch. He swung the sling around his head. When he released one end of it, the projectile went whizzing through space. It barely missed the mark.

"Damn! I'm *really* out of practice. Let me try again." This time, as he was successful, he went strutting around like an Andean cock-of-the-rock, all the while chanting, "Oh, yeah, I'm the best! Oh, yeah, ... !" The boys spent the rest of the afternoon hurling missiles at their target.

* * *

They stayed at the administrative center for several days. Right before resuming their travels, they had an unexpected visitor. It was a *chaski* with a message. He was, in fact, the last of a whole relay of runners who had brought news from the next Inka center to the south. When the *chaski* arrived at Catarpe, he was completely out of breath, having sprinted a half-mile. He was dressed in a plain tunic. His mantle snaked over one shoulder and under the opposite arm. The two ends were tied together at his chest. On his feet were tough llama-hide sandals with soles of double thickness, in his left hand a sling, and in his right a trumpet made from a large conch shell. While working, he employed the trumpet to alert the next runner in the chain that he was on his way.

Seeing the Inka official, he panted, "Sir ... a word with you ... if you please." Going up to the man, he bowed stiffly and announced,

"I'm sorry to have to tell you this. It's no longer possible to follow the imperial highway on this side of the mountains. To the south, a volcano's erupting. It's spewing out a huge cloud of ash. The winds are pushing the cloud westward. The road and everything else is being blanketed. Some days the cloud's so thick you can't see the sun."

"How do you suggest we bypass this volcano?" demanded the official.

"The best course of action would be to take a detour. From here you can follow a transverse road over the Andes to the eastern highway. You can proceed along it to Kulli-Wasi. Then you can return to the western side."

"Okay, that's what we'll do."

* * *

The Catarpe oasis sustained a variety of creatures, including vicuñas. Walking along the transverse road to the east of the settlement, the boys saw large herds of the animal. The vicuñas were grazing on the lush grasses that grew around seeps and springs in the area. They were much smaller than their cousins, the llamas and alpacas, standing only four *k'apas*—the distance across an outstretched hand, from the tip of the thumb to the tip of the little finger, so about nine inches—high at the shoulder. The fur on their upper bodies was a light cinnamon color. Their bellies and legs were white. It was the eight-year-old's impression that they were shy and constantly alert to danger. Whenever the children tried to sneak up on them, their heads shot up. They emitted high-pitched whistles and disappeared.

K'uchi-Wara said, "My dad told me that the Inkas don't let people hunt vicuñas. The animals can't be harmed at all. But every four years, they're rounded up, sheared, and released. Their wool's the finest in the land. It's used to make clothing for the king and his family. By law, nobody else is allowed to wear such clothes. And anyone caught breaking the law is executed. I hear that it's a *horrible* death!"

As the group made their way to the continental divide, they ascended a broad valley completely covered with scree. There were no plants, no animals. The grasses and vicuñas had been left behind at the oasis. In this part of the Atacama, where the sun is relentless and it rarely rains, no water is to be found. They trudged along in a parched sea, the long ridges of fractured rock like fossilized waves stretching away to infinity. The bleakness and monotony of the landscape was broken only by the mountains and volcanoes that towered over them toward the north and south.

After crossing the divide, the only difference they noticed was that they were descending rather than ascending. The scenery remained the same. One afternoon, heading down a gently sloping plain of rubble, they came upon an assembly of stone giants. The figures were distorted and grotesque. Almost seventy *k'apas* (fifty feet) high, they had been sculpted by the wind over many years. The priests honored these strange stones as *waqas*.

It was only a few days later that they found themselves traversing an enormous salt-flat. There was salt, nothing but salt, as far as K'uchi-Wara could see. And given that the land was perfectly level, he could see quite a ways. The salt-flat was completely sterile.

The eight-year-old was walking with Qispi and Waman. Turning to the priest, he said, "Now I understand why some of the llamas had to be loaded up with grass. There's nothing for them to eat here."

"That's right," came the response. "There's no drinking water either, which is why we've had to bring extra."

"Do you get the feeling that we're just walking in place?" K'uchi-Wara asked his companions.

"Yeah!" said Qispi. "We've been going for a long long time. And as far as I can tell, we haven't gotten anywhere."

"The landscape's totally featureless," explained Waman. "So we have no way to measure our progress. It's disorienting."

In the afternoon, clouds appeared. They began to build vertically and to merge until the whole sky was a dark grey. As the first cold drops fell, the three drew their mantles over their heads and tightly about their shoulders. There was no place to take shelter, so they continued walking.

"Isn't it odd to get a shower here?" asked K'uchi-Wara.

"I guess so," said Waman. "But it *does* happen."

After a while, the rain ceased. The eight-year-old looked up and all around. He halted, completely awestruck.

"What is it?" asked Waman. Then he too stopped. "*Añau!*" was all he managed to say as he scanned his surroundings.

During the rainstorm, a thin film of water had covered the salt-flat, turning it into a giant mirror. As K'uchi-Wara gazed across the land, he saw the flawless image of a blue sky in which floated clouds that were piled up like mighty mountains.

"I can't tell where the salt-flat ends and the sky begins," said Qispi.

"I know what you mean," affirmed Waman. "I feel like I'm suspended between heaven and earth."

Without warning, the eight-year-old raised both arms and started flapping them as if they were wings. Then he went running around and yelling at the top of his lungs, "I'M A CONDOR! I'M A CONDOR, SOARING IN THE BLUE!"

Qispi joined in the fun. As the priest watched them, he shook his head and uttered, "How sad. The *qhapaq huchas* have gone raving mad. That said, they really *do* look like they're flying!"

By the time the party reached the Inka highway on the eastern slope of the Andes, the greenery had returned. The plants—and more generally, the environment—on this side were somehow different than on the western side. Although still desert, it did not seem as dry, nor as harsh. There were scrubby thorn-bushes and many kinds of cactus. To K'uchi-Wara, the most impressive cacti were the *cardón*, green candelabra forty *k'apas* (thirty feet) high and twelve *k'apas* (nine feet) in circumference. Some of them had a dozen or more arms. Along with the flora there was fauna, including herds of vicuñas.

* * *

Day by day, the boys walked side by side. As they walked, there was one idea that was always on their minds. Although it usually stayed at the subconscious level, sometimes it could not be suppressed, and intruded into their conscious thoughts. But even when they became aware of it, they did not talk about it. They considered the idea taboo. That did not, however, stop each child from mulling it over in his brain. What was the idea that so obsessed them? DEATH.

K'uchi-Wara wondered, *What's it like to die? Does it hurt? Or is it like sleeping, only without the dreams? If it's like sleep, do you wake from death? I guess not. I helped Dad and the uncles to slaughter those llamas and alpacas. And once the animals were dead, they stayed dead. They didn't wake up.*

Dad once said that all living things die. I ... suppose ... that's true. The mummies sitting in their chullpas *at the top of the pass—my ancestors ... they all died. The bones that Qispi and I found from the thousands of traitors ... they all died. In the dream I had at the foot of Putina Volcano, where I came face-to-face with those* qhapaq huchas ... *they all died. And they were kids, just like me. So am I going to die? I used to think that only old and sick people die. But not my parents, not my friends, and certainly not me! Was I wrong? Could it be that someday I—this mind housed in this body, the person who's thinking these thoughts, ME—will die?* K'uchi-Wara shuddered.

Maybe the Inkas have the right idea of death. They say that when you die, you go to a better world. That'd be nice. Then again, what could be better than this world? My parents are here. So are Jukumari and Nina and Qispi and Waman and my alpacas.

* * *

In Qispi's mind, Death was a shadowy figure. *He comes to get you when you don't expect it. So you've got to be smart. You should always be on the lookout for Him. My ancestors probably forgot that rule. That's why they died. One day they got careless and didn't watch out for Him. They ended up as mummies in the cave near our village.*

If Death comes for me, I'll run and hide. I'm pretty good at hiding, so I don't think He'll find me. But suppose He does? What will happen then? Will my parents or K'uchi-Wara be able to save me? If I kick and scream and bite Him, will He let me go?

Sometimes Death does awful things to people. There was that old man who lived down the street from us. When Death took him, he looked like a skeleton. He was mostly skin and bones. He also smelled bad and had sores all over his arms and legs. Maybe that's what's going to happen to me.

Or how about when the Old One sacrificed the llama to Putina. The animal started to struggle as blood squirted from its throat. Everything got splattered with red. Then the llama crapped all over and stopped moving. I don't want that to happen to me.

* * *

Although neither boy fully understood his fate, the fact that each succeeding day brought him closer and closer to that fate produced a growing anxiousness. In turn, the anxiousness gave rise to tension between them.

It was afternoon when the children came across the carcass of a vicuña that had died of natural causes. The dry air had mummified its remains. They reached down and ran their fingers through its long fleece. It felt silky and lustrous and fine. Acting on a sudden impulse, K'uchi-Wara turned to his friend and blurted out, "This is what *you're* going to look like very soon. After the Inkas sacrifice you, you're going to become a dried out husk. Just like the vicuña!"

"Huh? What're you talking about?"

"Your eyes are going to shrivel up like *chuño*. Then they'll fall out of their sockets. Your body's going to wither until it looks like a dirty old rag. Your penis is going to shrink to the size of a peanut. Your balls will become like dry corn kernels."

"That's not true! Why're you saying these things? You're *crazy!* What've I done to you?"

K'uchi-Wara was on a roll. He could not stop himself. "After you've become a mummy, they're going to stick you in the ground. It's going to be pitch-black down there. You're going to be cold and alone and *scared*. And your friends and family are going to *forget* you."

"That's a LIE!" screamed Qispi, tears streaming down his face. "So j–just shut up!"

"You can't make me!" the eight-year-old retorted. "Besides, it's true. Just you wait and see!" As he said these words, tears welled up in his own eyes.

K'uchi-Wara was miserable for the rest of the day. Although he experienced a little remorse for having taunted his friend, he mostly felt sorry for himself.

When the boy's father found out how badly his son had behaved, he became angry. He made K'uchi-Wara apologize to Qispi. But that only caused the eight-year-old to resent the six-year-old, even though it was the younger child who had been wronged.

* * *

That night, in the privacy of their lodging-house room, the parents conferred. "I don't know what's gotten into the boy," said his father. "I thought he and Qispi were friends."

"They are," replied the mother. "K'uchi-Wara's acting up because he's worried. And he's frustrated because he's not sure how to handle his emotions. But you would know that if you bothered to *talk* to your son!"

"I *do* talk to him."

"No! I mean really *com-mu-ni-cate* with him. Right now he needs your guidance and reassurance. You need to spend *more* time with him and *less* time with the Inkas."

* * *

Within a week of leaving Catarpe, the party arrived at Kulli-Wasi, an Inka outpost in a native village.

"Dad," K'uchi-Wara asked, "why is the place called 'purple house'?"

"I've no idea. I'm sure we'll find out, though."

The hamlet was nondescript, consisting of a dense collection of circular and elliptical buildings. They were made of fieldstones and had thatched roofs. They were haphazardly spread across the valley floor. In the middle of the jumble of buildings, one structure stood out. Situated by itself at the top of a knoll, it dominated the rest of the village. It was surrounded by a perimeter wall that partly obscured it. From what K'uchi-Wara could see of it, however, the building had two striking features: it was rectangular in shape, and pinkish-purple in color.

The Old One led the group through a maze of streets. As they went, he shouted at the local folks, "Avert your eyes! Avert your eyes! *Qhapaq huchas* passing by!" The weary travelers walked up the hillock and slipped through a narrow gate in the wall, where they saw the Kulli-Wasi in its entirety.

Qispi exclaimed, "*Achalau*–how pretty!"

The Kulli-Wasi was not large, measuring eleven by four paces. It was constructed of sandstone blocks. Typical of Inka architecture, it had a trapezoidal door and trapezoidal niches set into the walls. It was occupied by a *kuraka*, an ally of the Inkas. He greeted them warmly. Like his residence, the local lord was a sight to see, being flamboyantly dressed in a green tunic to which red and yellow feathers had been sewn. On his shoulders was a light mantle, on his feet moccasins. What astonished K'uchi-Wara most of all, though, was his headdress, which consisted of a woven band of red and green that had been wrapped multiple times around his head to create a turban. Stuck into the front of the turban was a feather of beaten gold. The feather was so thin and delicate that it quivered whenever the *kuraka* moved his head.

The lord honored his guests with a feast. They dined on the patio, seated on low stools, and protected from prying eyes by the surrounding wall. They ate their fill of roasted guinea pig, maize cooked with herbs and chili peppers, local greens, and cactus fruit. There also was a never-ending supply of *chicha*.

The state official sat next to the boy's father, discussing his favorite topic: the Inkas' administrative genius. He was saying, "Here we rule indirectly, through the *kuraka*. To the extent possible, we try to aggrandize him in the eyes of his people. That way, he can exercise more control over them. That's why we built the Kulli-Wasi ..."

Later, when the party withdrew to the inside of the Purple-House, K'uchi-Wara remained outside. *I want to have fun with kids my own age. But not with Qispi. I've had enough of him! So what if the Old One catches me? There's not a lot he can do to punish me!* He snuck through the gate and out of the compound, which was easy to do as there were no guards. Then he ran down the knoll to the village.

K'uchi-Wara met up with some street-urchins. Because he had difficulty understanding them, their conversation involved repetition, gesticulation, and pantomime.

"Hi. My name's K'uchi-Wara. Can I play with you?"

"I don't see why not," said a boy of ten. He appeared to be the leader.

"Who are you?" asked a girl. "I don't remember seeing you before. Where'd you come from?"

"Hold on," said another boy. "Aren't you with the group that arrived today? You're one of those *special* kids, aren't you?"

"How would you know that?" asked the ten-year-old, "since you're not supposed to look at their faces!"

"Obviously, I peeked!" said the other, grinning. "But that means we can't be seen with you, K'uchi-Wara. We'd get in trouble!"

"*Ux*—of course, you can! Do I have a scarlet fringe on my forehead? NO! Do I look like a great lord? NO! I'm just the same as you!"

It was no use, the other children were already scattering. K'uchi-Wara had rarely felt so alone. Head down, he trudged up the hillock.

From the Kulli-Wasi, the group crossed the Andes again, returning to the western highway. It was a beautiful day as they made their way along an avenue of volcanoes. One of them had erupted violently in the past. It had ejected cinder and pumice from its crater, chunks of which littered the ground for *tupus* around. K'uchi-Wara picked up a piece of pumice. It had a rough texture, its surface pitted with tiny holes. *This rock's mostly empty space. It weighs nothing. I imagine it would even float on water.* He went over to a pumice boulder and kicked it. It moved, having a feather's weight. He picked it up and hoisted it over his head. "LOOK AT ME!" he shouted to the others. "I'm the *strongest* kid in the whole kingdom!"

"*Ahau!*" roared Qispi, delighted with K'uchi-Wara's antics. "How funny!"

The rest of the party, with the exception of the Old One, laughed as well. As the eight-year-old watched the younger boy, he began to smile. And just like that, they were reconciled.

In the evening, as the family supped, K'uchi-Wara's mother noticed that her son had ripped his black tunic. It was the one she had given him before their departure from Wila-Nayra. "Silly boy! What've you done to your tunic?"

"Nothing ... oh, *that*! I guess I tore it on the sharp rock I was playing with today."

"If you'll take it off, I'll mend it for you," she told him.

"Ma'am," Waman protested, "that's such a menial task. I can get one of the attendants to do it. After all, that's what they're here for!"

"But *I* want to do it!" she insisted. "Anything for my child."

* * *

It was a day like any other in the desert. As nothing seemed to change in that wasteland—and as it was impossible to distinguish one diurnal cycle from another—K'uchi-Wara didn't realize he had reached a milestone: he had been on the road for eighteen weeks and had taken almost 4 million steps.

The boy was walking along, listening to the crunch, crunch, crunch of his heavily calloused feet on the gravel. His steps were necessarily quick because the ground had been baking in the sun, which beat down from above. The air was so dry that his sweat evaporated immediately from his skin. It was so stifling that every time he took a breath he thought he would suffocate. He surveyed the tortured terrain to the west, shimmering in the heat. The light reflecting off the dun-colored land made him squint. In the distance rose fractured hills that appeared to be little more than heaps of burnt slag and ash. They looked like they had been formed in the heart of a great forge.

The child addressed the desert, which he thought of as a living thing. *You don't care about me or the other people, do you? If I died here, you wouldn't even notice. And everything would be the same as before. The sun would still shine. The wind would still blow. The mountains to the east would still look down on the land. I wish I were somewhere else. Anywhere!* K'uchi-Wara imagined himself back home in Wila-Nayra. He was making his way through a sea of bunchgrass, clumps of slender green stems reaching to his waist and topped by feathery heads of silver. The heads bobbed up and down in the cool breeze. He came over a rise ... and look! There was Jukumari, his bulky frame unmistakable. He was herding a large flock of alpacas. Among the animals was K'uchi-Wara's favorite female with her baby, suckling at her teat. Going up to her, he ran his hand through her silky white fleece. He gazed into a blue eye. An overpowering wave of nostalgia and loss swept over him. He felt like crying. He missed his alpacas and his cousin and his homeland. Would he ever see them again?

Lost in thought, K'uchi-Wara tripped and fell. His knee slammed into a jagged rock, slicing it open. *"AYAYAU!"* he yelled. He tried to stand on the injured leg as blood streamed down it. It buckled under him and he fell again. As he lay there, his parents ran over to him, with Waman close behind. Worry in their eyes and voices, they all started talking at once: "What happened? Are you okay? Does it hurt? Can you walk? My poor child."

Waman took charge of the boy's treatment. While the parents looked on, he stopped a pack animal. He removed a bundle of cotton-gauze from the large bag that hung at its side. He wadded some of the gauze and pressed it against the gash. K'uchi-Wara flinched. Waman continued applying pressure until he had stopped the bleeding. Then he cleaned the wound as best he could with water, and bound it with clean gauze. Completing the job, he gave the child a smile and said, "That ought to do it! In a few days, you'll be as good as new. In the meantime, you'll have to be carried."

Later that afternoon, Qispi sidled up to K'uchi-Wara, who was being borne by an attendant. "Well, aren't *you* the great lord," the six-year-old teased. "You don't have to walk like the rest of us! Maybe we can find a litter for you. Then you can *really* ride in comfort."

"Oh, shut up! Do you really think I fell on purpose? So I wouldn't have to walk? K'uchi-Wara was annoyed by the boy's ribbing. On the other hand, he didn't mind the attention, which distracted him from the throbbing of his knee.

* * *

During the day, it was blistering in the direct sunlight. As soon as the sun set, however, the temperature plummeted, there being little moisture in the air to trap the heat. The dryness of the atmosphere together with the darkness of the nights meant the stars were incredibly bright in the Atacama. After a long hard day on the road, Waman loved to sit outside a *tampu*, staring at the heavens. He would see a luminous band, which appeared to be made up of countless stars, arching across the firmament. "*Atakachau!*" he would exclaim. "What a pleasure to see the Cosmic River!"

One night, as he relaxed beneath the open sky, he began to think. *Is it really fair for us to sacrifice K'uchi-Wara? He's a good kid. Doesn't he deserve the chance to grow up? Shouldn't he be able to live in peace in his homeland, herding his beloved alpacas? I understand he had a little girlfriend. They ought to be able to marry, have children, and grow old together.*

What about K'uchi-Wara's parents? They seem like decent folk. What right do we have to take their son from them? The prospect of us offering up the boy seems to be affecting them differently. Outwardly the mother has always been courteous, though aloof. Inwardly I suspect that she mistrusts and despises us. Who could blame her? After all, we're going to sacrifice her baby! The father's harder to read. I don't think he's quite as hostile toward us. And though I'm sure he hates the idea of our taking his son, he also sees the advantages in it. But I get the impression that the parents' differing attitudes towards us is starting to put a strain on their marriage. At times they seem curt with each other.

I wonder what would happen if we were to offer up llamas instead of K'uchi-Wara? Would Mount Titi-Urqu be offended? Would the waqa withhold rain from the surrounding area? Would it stop the local llamas from breeding? I don't know for sure, but I doubt it. What can I do, though? I'm just a junior priest. And the Old One—what a great name the boys have thought up for him, and a fitting one too—is determined to sacrifice him.

* * *

Waman was not the only one to enjoy the heavens after sundown. It being a fine night, K'uchi-Wara's mother asked her son to accompany her outside so they could look at the stars together. They sat down, side by side, resting their backs comfortably against a big rock. She said, "It won't be long before we reach our destination. We should try to spend as much time together as possible." They both gazed upward.

The air was transparent. High above the surface-world, another one met their eyes, very wondrous, where large black patches or silhouettes floated against the brightness of the Milky Way.

"Do you remember those nights in Wila-Nayra? When your father and I would take you outside to teach you our sky lore?"

"Of course, though it seems like *ages* ago. It was always a lot of fun."

"We didn't do it *just* to entertain you. We thought you should know about the upper world since it mirrors our own. And since it can affect our lives. Did any of what we taught you stick with you?"

"Why don't you test me?"

"Okay." Pointing skyward, she said, "See the big black shape?"

"You mean that one?"

"No, not there. Follow my hand. Yes, there. What's that 'dark constellation' called?"

"Umm ... give me a hint."

"You can see legs, a large body, a long neck, and a head with two bright stars. It seems to be quietly eyeing us."

"Oh yeah, *that's* the Great Llama."

"Right. Underneath the Great Llama is a slightly smaller patch? What's that?"

"I know! It's the Baby Llama, suckling at its mama's teat."

"Good. What can you tell me about those constellations?"

"What do you mean?"

"Why are they important? Why did we bother to teach you about them?"

"Uhh ... because when we honor them, they make our herds grow. Right?"

"Of course."

"Now I have a question for you," said the boy. "If the Great Llama gives animals more babies, what constellation does that for people?"

"Do you remember Qutu? Too bad it's not visible tonight. It's the tiny constellation with seven stars."

"Sure."

"Well, people can increase their numbers by making offerings to it."

"I have another question. During my First Haircutting, Uncle chose a star to be my astral-twin. It's supposed to be tied to my happiness. I always forget which one it is. Do you know?"

The woman scanned the heavens, then pointed to a reddish pin-prick of light. "I think it's that one. Pretty, isn't it?"

As K'uchi-Wara gazed up at it, he said to himself, *I'm counting on you, little star, to bring me good luck!*

"So, do you agree that it's important to know about the night sky?"

"Sure, Mom. Whatever you say."

"Good. Then our night sessions weren't a complete waste of time. Come here and give your mother a hug."

* * *

After crossing the Atacama for what seemed to the children to be a lifetime, the group finally reached the Copiapó Valley. That's where the desert ends. They were *ecstatic* to see some greenery again.

It was evening. The boys were feeling restless and bored. They had just arrived at the *tampu* where the party would overnight. Being careful not to let the Old One see them, they helped the llama drivers to unload the pack animals. Then each one grabbed a woolen sack and dragged it into a storeroom. K'uchi-Wara was about to dump his burden, when he realized what it contained: the clothing and other items that he and Qispi had been given in Cuzco for their sacrifices. He had never seen his friend's effects. Thus they decided to play their own version of "dress-up." They untied the string that bound the bag's opening and removed some of its contents. Although the Old One had never told them *not* to look at these items, they were excited because it seemed like they were breaking a taboo. The older boy laid out the articles he had received. They included the pair of moccasins, headdress of condor feathers, headband, pendant, and silver bracelet. He donned them. "How do I look?"

"*Kusa*—great!"

"This is the costume of a mighty lord from Qulla-Suyu. *Bow* to me!"

The younger child howled with laughter. "Now it's *my* turn!"

As K'uchi-Wara pulled articles from the sack, Qispi put them on. He placed a heavy necklace of Spondylus shell, lapis lazuli, and malachite beads around his neck, and wrapped an oversized loincloth about his hips. Then he donned a half dozen cotton tunics decorated with stylized birds and fish, before slipping into a pair of sandals. As a final touch, the eight-year-old set a crown of yellow and black feathers on his head.

"There! How do *I* look?"

"Terrific! Wearing so many clothes, you look like a fat mummy-bundle. The Inkas don't have to sacrifice you. All they have to do is leave you like that, and you'll sweat to death!"

Qispi smiled wistfully.

A voice echoed through the room. "WHAT'S going on in here?" The boys jumped. But it was only Waman. He was horrified to see the sacrificial clothing strewn about the place. "Is this how you treat your gifts from the king? What in Inti's name are you thinking?" The children bowed their heads. He continued, "You're lucky the Old One didn't catch you. He'd severely punish you!" As he pronounced these words, he stooped down to pick up a tunic, carefully folding it.

* * *

Later Waman continued to dwell on the incident. *What were the boys thinking? The items they were playing with are sacred! They're not toys. I'm sure that K'uchi-Wara was the instigator of the trouble. No matter what he suggests they do, Qispi goes along with it. Was K'uchi-Wara just being a kid? Or was he subconsciously acting up? Maybe the Old One's right. Maybe the boy is struggling with his emotions, trying to come to grips with the idea of his own death. It would make sense. He is, after all, still a child. And I don't think he fully understands what's going to happen to him. So, what should I do about it? Tell the Old One? No, he'd overreact. I'll try to treat K'uchi-Wara with greater understanding. I'll give him the time and space he needs to work things out for himself.*

* * *

The farther south the travelers went, the greener the landscape became. In early November, spring in the southern hemisphere, they reached the Aconcagua Valley in central Chile. They had left the Atacama Desert far behind. They had entered a region with a relatively mild climate and comparatively lush vegetation. Following the royal road up a flat-topped hill, they came to an Inka administrative center called Mercachas. Before entering it, K'uchi-Wara and his parents stood at the apex of the hill and looked out over the valley. They exclaimed in unison, "*Añañau*—wow!" They had never seen anything like it. The boy had spent his whole life on the side of a mountain where no trees grow. Although during his journey he had come across isolated trees, most of them had been stunted and gnarled, with branches deformed by the wind. He had never laid eyes on ones that were, at least by comparison, so tall and majestic. And he certainly had not seen a whole forest!

The Inkas had located Mercachas at the intersection of two major highways: the north-south one that the group was following, and a transverse route leading over the Andes into Argentina. From this royal center, they could control traffic along both roads. They also could dominate the people living in the Aconcagua Valley. The architecture there was typical, consisting of rectangular buildings set around patios.

K'uchi-Wara was sad to learn that Mercachas was nearly the "end of the road," both in a literal and a figurative sense, for Qispi. The younger child would remain at the administrative center until late December. Then he would participate in the festival of Qhapaq Raymi. Afterwards he would be taken along the west-east road to a high peak in Argentina. There—wearing the necklace, loincloth, cotton tunics, sandals, and feather headdress—he would be sacrificed. The name of the mountain where he would meet his end was Aconcagua, the same as the valley.

K'uchi-Wara and his parents stayed at Mercachas for a week. All too soon, however, it was time to leave. As the boys said their goodbyes and embraced, they were trembling with emotion. Qispi had tears in his eyes. They had been together for many months and had shared many adventures. Each one knew he would never see his friend again. But there was more to it: deep down, they both realized that they were intimately connected by a common fate, which they would soon meet.

An Inka official at the administrative center in the Mapocho Valley

Chapter Twelve: Empire's Edge

It's only eight and a half *tupus* (forty miles) as the crow flies between the Aconcagua and the Mapocho Valleys. K'uchi-Wara and his folks covered the distance in a few days. By the time they reached the Mapocho, they had been traveling for over twenty-six weeks. The parents had experienced this period as tomorrows becoming todays, and todays becoming yesterdays, as one diurnal cycle after another had passed in long and tedious succession. The child had felt the time go by in a more dramatic way. Being much younger, it seemed to him that he had been marching day in and day out for his entire life; that he had been on the go for all the days of the world. So many, in fact, that they had begun to crowd one another and to pile up, until he had lost track of them. Was today the first of the month? Or the last? Who knew? What did it matter?

It was nearly the end of his journey. K'uchi-Wara could hardly believe that he had walked 440 *tupus* (2,050 miles). When he had taken his first step upon leaving Cuzco, little had he known that he would have to take another *five and a half million* before he reached the Mapocho Valley. But it may have been better that he had *not* known. Otherwise he would have been overwhelmed and demoralized by the sheer magnitude of what was expected of him. Such is often the case with projects we undertake in life: if we knew at the outset how involved they would be or how long they would take, we would never start them.

* * *

In the Mapocho Valley there was an Inka settlement and administrative center. During the next five hundred years, it would grow into a major metropolis spread over a huge area. Within what would become Santiago's city limits, the child and his entourage followed a road that would come to be known as Independence Avenue. In the part of town where the Mapocho train station would be located, they passed a *tampu* and walked toward the southeast, crossing the Mapocho River by means of a small bridge. The Inka settlement sat at the foot of Huelén Hill, where Santiago's main square is now situated.

K'uchi-Wara was treated like a celebrity. The day after his arrival, he, his mother, and father were given a tour of the administrative center. They found the architecture to be typically Inka, consisting of rectangular buildings arranged around plazas. It differed from the architecture they had seen elsewhere, however, in the way the buildings were constructed. In northern Chile, structures were usually made of fieldstones set in mortar. In the Mapocho, they consisted of large wooden posts that were driven into the ground, to which walls of wattle and daub were attached. A fine plaster was added to the walls, and the roofs were thatched.

The dignitary leading their tour took the child and his parents along a winding path to the top of Huelén Hill. There the Inkas had built a ceremonial platform. As the eight-year-old scrambled up onto the platform and looked south, he was treated to a spectacular view of the valley. Like the Aconcagua, it was wooded. There were oaks, beeches, soapbark trees, and a variety of evergreens. The Mapocho River was a silver ribbon running down the middle of the valley, which was circled by a chain of rugged hills.

Sweeping the forest with his eyes, K'uchi-Wara spotted occasional gaps. In their midst, he could make out tiny buildings and agricultural plots. "Who lives *there*?" he asked.

"Each clearing's occupied by a Pecunche family," the dignitary said. "The Pecunche are the native inhabitants of this region. They're such a *primitive* people! You can see they don't live in hamlets, but are spread out across the landscape. Their houses are simple. The walls are made of wattle and daub, hay, or animal skins. They raise corn and a few other crops."

A monumental peak dominated the vista from Huelén Hill. On its upper slopes was a rounded ice cap that from a distance looked smooth, ample, and white—a Chachapoya maiden's breast. On top of the dome was a pyramid of reddish-brown rock—the nipple. Dazzled, the boy blurted out, "What mountain is *that*?"

"That's Titi-Urqu. The *waqa* you'll soon be serving. But first, we'll have to get you up there!"

"How're you going to do that? It looks mighty big."

"Don't worry. When the time comes, we'll make sure you get there safely."

"That's exactly what I'm worried about,"mumbled the mother.

"How will you know when it's time for me to go to Titi-Urqu?" K'uchi-Wara persisted.

"My goodness, you're inquisitive. Our calendar will tell us when the time's right. You know how the Inka calendar works, don't you?"

The child shook his head.

"No? I'm surprised. I thought everyone knew. Hmm ... how best to explain it. Every morning before dawn, a priest comes up here and watches the sun rise. On the June solstice, he'll see the first rays of light coming from behind Mount Muru ('bald')." He pointed at a high peak to the north that looked like a bald head. "Each succeeding day, he'll observe the sun move little by little toward the south. On the equinox, the solar disk will appear from behind Ch'unpi ('brown'), the mountain over there." He indicated a large dun-colored peak with neither vegetation nor snow on it. "On the December solstice, the priest will see the sun rising from behind Titi-Urqu. Then the sun will begin its six-month journey northward. Does that make sense?"

The boy nodded.

"Good! You leave for Titi-Urqu after Qhapaq Raymi. The festival takes place around the December solstice."

*   *   *

As a celebrity, K'uchi-Wara was introduced to other important people. One sunny afternoon, he and his parents met the Inka governor of the province. The man's name was Vitacura. The first thing the child noticed about Vitacura were his garments, which were like those worn by the Apu-Panaka, and which denoted his high status. His tunic was deep blue with large red diamonds, arranged end to end, circling the waistline. In the middle of each large diamond was a smaller one in yellow, and an even tinier one in white. Completing the man's outfit were a mantle, sandals, bracelet, ear-spools, headband, and a feather panache attached to the front of the band. His hair was short.

Standing in the courtyard of his residence, Vitacura held a monologue with his three visitors. He explained to them that, unlike the typical governor, he lacked the broad powers to oversee everything in his province, which was quite unfortunate. "I mostly exercise authority over the *mitmaq-kuna* in the Mapocho and Aconcagua Valleys," he told them. "The majority of settlers are Diaguita. They were transplanted from the Copiapó area. You must have passed through their lands on your way south from Cuzco. We employ some *mitmaq-kuna* in the local mines. We use other settlers to man the forts, the most important one being Chena. It guards the southern entrance to the Mapocho Valley. The Diaguita garrison is vital for stopping hostile groups from invading. Most of the *mitmaq-kuna*, though, have been put to work farming. They produce enough food to feed not only themselves, but the miners, the garrisons, and all the Inka administrators ..."

The child glanced at his parents. Whereas his father seemed to be listening to the man, his mother looked stony-faced and bored. For his part, he had met far too many Inka officials and had heard enough speeches to last a lifetime. His eyes glazed over, his mind wandered. *I wonder what Jukumari and Nina are up to? Let's see. If I know the "Bear," he's probably out herding. He's sitting at one of the pools above Wila-Nayra. He's dangling his feet in the cool water and watching his herd of alpacas. The animals are grazing happily and humming. I hope he doesn't have to fight any pumas, since he's not very good with the sling. What would my little "Fire" be doing now? She's most likely with her mother, who's showing her how to use a backstrap loom. Nina's making herself a cloth bag. It's decorated with red, green, purple, and beige stripes. She's such a spirited girl, I'll bet she's giving her mother a hard time. At this very instant, both Jukumari and Nina are asking themselves where I am. And what I'm doing. I'd give anything to see them, if only for a moment.*

K'uchi-Wara's mind returned to the present. His father was asking Vitacura a question. "Why go through the trouble of bringing laborers here? Wouldn't it be easier to put the local people to work?"

"You'd think so, wouldn't you? But the Pecunche are a wild and unruly people. They have no formal government. And they don't know how to serve. While it's been hard to impose our authority over them, it's been nearly impossible to get them to work."

On another occasion, K'uchi-Wara met Michimalonko, the local chief. He appeared to be in his late twenties, though it was hard to tell his exact age. He was powerfully built, with broad shoulders and a barrel chest. What fired up the boy's imagination, however, was the man's face. On the left side of it was a scarlet-colored worm that ran from the temple to the mouth. *He looks like a real savage. And the scar he's got is amazing! Horrifying too! I don't want to be rude, but I can't help staring at it. It looks like he got it recently. I wonder how? Maybe in a knife fight with another savage. He probably killed the other man!*

Michimalonko was accompanied by a teenage girl. The boy assumed that she was his wife. They wore the simple garb of the Pecunche: a pair of rectangular textiles woven from wool. Whereas one piece was wrapped around the waist like a skirt and fastened by a belt, the other was thrown loosely over the shoulders as a mantle. The girl's mantle was open in front and K'uchi-Wara could see her bare breasts. Both Michimalonko and his wife had long black hair that hung down their backs.

It was Vitacura who introduced the boy to the Pecunche chief. "Here's the *qhapaq hucha* we're sending to Titi-Urqu in the name of the king. What do you think?"

Michimalonko inspected the child as if he were a llama for trade, and replied in perfect Quechua, "Yes, he'll do. I hope that with this offering, Titi-Urqu ends the drought. Our corn's wilting." Then the chief addressed K'uchi-Wara directly. "Little one, aren't you excited? Soon you'll be with our *waqa*."

"I guess so."

Michimalonko and the girl left shortly thereafter, the latter not having spoken a word. Once they were gone, Vitacura's attitude toward them seemed to change. "*Atatau!* The man's a barbarian! He insists that he controls all the land between the Aconcagua and Mapocho Valleys. But who knows if it's true. He asserts that he governs the local people. I've seen no evidence of it, though. And he claims to be our friend. But I don't trust him at all. If he had an army, he'd drive us from the region so fast ... and what about the woman. Did you see her clothes?" he asked nobody in particular. "Unlike Inka ladies, who are paragons of *virtue*, their women have no shame. Imagine going about with your tits uncovered!"

Why's he making such a fuss? K'uchi-Wara wondered. *Hasn't he ever seen a mother feeding her baby? Nobody would care if you exposed yourself like that in Wila-Nayra. Considering the cold and wind, though, you might end up with frostbite or windburn!*

The governor hadn't finished his rant. "I can't *wait* to escape this backwater and return to Cuzco! If I were to leave these uncouth lice-infested *savages* today, it wouldn't be too soon! But I have an obligation to king and country." With these words, he seemed to run out of steam.

* * *

While the family had been on the road, walking about two and a half *tupus* each day, they had had neither the time nor energy to dwell on the sacrifice. But now that they had reached the Mapocho Valley and had more opportunity for reflection, they could no longer suppress their anxiety and anger. K'uchi-Wara noticed a growing tension between his parents. Whereas outwardly they appeared calm and cool, he could tell that on the inside they were becoming more and more distressed. When they were together, they seemed excessively formal and courteous. It was as if each feared he might upset the other and start a fight.

K'uchi-Wara sat up on the sleeping-platform. It was the middle of the night. In the next room—his family occupied a suite of rooms in an Inka building—he heard loud voices.

"The Inkas are *monsters!*" his mother raged. "That's the only way to describe them. Only a monster would rip a child from his mother's arms, take him to a mountain, and offer him up."

"We've been over this a thousand times," the boy heard his father say. He sounded tired. "I agree with you, they *are* monsters!"

The woman's anger would not be soothed. "I nourished the seed for nine months, while it developed in my belly. I suckled the babe at my teats for two years as it grew. After the boy's First Haircutting, I fed him for six years. All the while, he matured and became a *real* person. That makes him the blood of my blood, the flesh of my flesh. And when he's gone, it'll leave a hole in my bosom that'll never be filled!"

"Why do you *always* make it sound like you're the only one who'll be affected by the sacrifice?" K'uchi-Wara could tell that his father was getting mad. "Who do you think planted the seed in your belly? Who supplied the food so you could feed the child? Who taught him the ways of the Lupaka so he could become a *real* person? He's a part of me too!"

"Okay, fine. It'll be a loss for you. But do you really think that your loss can compare with my *devastation*?"

"I'm *not* going to play your game of who-will-suffer-the-most. But just as motherhood defines you as a woman, so bloodline defines me as a nobleman. And when the boy is offered up, my lineage will be cut short. So, *yes!* My misfortune will be as great as yours."

"How do you figure?"

"What are you—a child?—that you don't understand the fundamentals of ancestry. Okay, let me explain them to you. I trace my roots back to the First Man. The Creator made him from clay, painted clothing on him, and breathed life into him...."

"That's *not* what I meant!"

"... From that remote time till today, the chain of descent has been unbroken...."

"Don't patronize me. I'm not a child. And I know *all about* your precious lineage."

" ... I'd hoped that between now and the distant future, the line of succession would *remain* unbroken, with K'uchi-Wara as a link. That's *not* to be, though."

"Your bloodline be damned! That's what I say! Damn the Inkas and your bloodline!"

"You scorn my ancestors. And you insult me. Not only do you insult me, but you, a woman, constantly question my authority."

Then K'uchi-Wara heard his mother shriek, "AUTHORITY? What authority? If you had any, you'd be able stand up to the Inkas. But since you don't, our son's going to be *sacrificed!*"

"Curse you! I also have a duty to the people of Wila-Nayra, all one hundred of them. As hard as it is to say, I won't see them killed to save one life. Not even if that life's more precious than my own!" With that, he stormed out of the room.

As the days passed, and the event drew closer and closer, it loomed larger and larger in the minds of the family members. Each one dealt with it in his own way. K'uchi-Wara had always thought of his mother as being self-assured. She seemed to cry often, though, being moved to tears by trivial things. Whereas during the journey south she had been content to let the attendants prepare their meals, she started cooking again. With a vengeance. Morning and night, she fixed her son's favorite foods. She would not accept help from anyone. In the Andes, to feed someone is to create a blood bond with them. She became increasingly protective of the boy too. When he left the house before dawn, she made sure his mantle was wrapped around his shoulders. When he fell and skinned his knee, she washed the wound and bandaged it. And when he ripped his clothes, she darned them.

After the last fight with his wife, K'uchi-Wara's father tried to stay out of her way. If they happened to end up in the same room, they rarely spoke. They barely looked at each other. At the same time, the man tried to be there for his son. "If you want to talk," he told the boy, "I'm always available."

K'uchi-Wara was worried about the approaching sacrifice. He was curious about it too. One way he dealt with his anxiety and curiosity was to hold long conversations with his father. He had no end of questions.

"How will it feel to die? Will it hurt?"

"No," his father replied. "You won't even notice when you slip from this world into the next one."

"What's the other world like? Is it the same as ours?"

"I suppose it's similar, though not exactly the same. For one thing, it's supposed to be very beautiful. Just imagine, you'll be living among the mountains. And there's nothing prettier in either world than a snow-capped peak at sunset! Life in the other world will be easier too. You'll never want for anything. You'll never feel hunger or thirst or cold or pain."

"I've always wondered what the mountain-*waqas* look like. Do you know?"

"Not really. But your grandfather used to say that they're tall and pale. They wear long white robes and carry a staff."

The child continued. "When I'm in the other world, will my body rot and stink?"

"No."

"Will my hair and fingernails keep growing?"

"I don't know."

"Will you miss me when I'm gone?"

The man looked his son in the eye. "That's a silly question. Of course,

I will! When you leave us, both your mother and I will feel the loss. Intensely! For the rest of our lives! I'm sure that your cousin Jukumari already misses you. And so does your friend, Nina."

K'uchi-Wara became obsessed with Titi-Urqu. Some days he would sit for long stretches of time on the platform atop Huelén Hill. He would gaze up at the mountain, studying its every feature. *It looks beautiful, but so cold.* The child also was preoccupied with the workings of the Inka calendar. He would wake up early each morning and stumble after Waman as they made their way along the winding path to the summit of Huelén. There they would watch the solar disk rise. They noted that little by little the sun was approaching the great bulk of Titi-Urqu.

* * *

K'uchi-Wara's father decided that for his son's sanity, and for his own, they *had* to get away from the administrative center, if only for a few days. So he asked Waman, who was always helpful, "Where should we go?"

The priest thought for a moment. Then he said, "I think K'uchi-Wara would enjoy seeing the Marga-Marga Gold Mine. It's very interesting. And it's not too far away. A trip there would *definitely* help him to take his mind off Titi-Urqu and the upcoming sacrifice. Yes, that's where *we'll* take him!"

"What do you mean 'we'?"

"I doubt the Old One would let you go alone—that is, without a priest. Someone to look after the child, to make sure he remains ritually pure. Come to think of it, I'm not sure the Old One would trust *me* with that type of responsibility!"

"Well, I trust you."

It was daybreak when K'uchi-Wara, his father, Waman, and a guide set off for the Marga-Marga Mine. They headed west. By evening they had reached a rustic hamlet, whose houses were little more than wooden shacks strung along the banks of a river. At this point in its course, the river was sluggish. Extensive gravel beds could be seen along its edge, while out in the middle, numerous sandbars poked out of the water.

"We're *here!*" Waman announced.

"We're *where?*" asked K'uchi-Wara.

"At our destination, of course. The *mine!*"

"But," the father protested, "I don't see any large open pits. If this is a mine, where does the gold-bearing ore come from?"

Waman smiled. "This is a placer mine."

"Huh?" said K'uchi-Wara.

"It's late now. I'll show you tomorrow."

They bedded down in one of the shacks. K'uchi-Wara found the sounds of the night—the lapping of water on rocks, the croaking of frogs, and the chirping of crickets, all of which were new to him—to be relaxing. He slept well.

He woke to a damp and foggy world, which was quite a change from the Atacama Desert. Dew covered everything. The trees surrounding the shack had become ghostly monsters. Puffs of mist wafted over the river, while overhead a thick blanket of fog reduced the sun to little more than a dim pastel-yellow circle. As the morning progressed, however, the circle grew in brightness and intensity of hue. Finally the sun burned away the fog, revealing a clear blue sky.

"Let's try our hand at finding gold, okay?" Waman said to K'uchi-Wara and his father.

"Oh, yes," replied the boy.

The three made their way down a muddy path from the shack to the river. Squelch, squelch, squelch went the child's feet as he walked through the thick mud. Evenly spaced along the water's edge were a large number of men. Raggedly dressed, they were squatting and holding large wooden bowls. Some spoke cheerfully to their neighbors, while others shouted good-naturedly to more distant friends. K'uchi-Wara didn't recognize the language.

"Who are they? Where are they from?" the child asked the priest.

"They're *mitmaq-kuna*. We brought them from the north to work as miners. They speak Diaguita."

"What are they doing?"

"Why, they're panning for gold. Let's see how they go about it."

Waman, the boy, and his father seated themselves on flat rocks and watched as one of the prospectors worked. He took his wooden bowl, which had a flat bottom and gently sloping sides, filled it halfway with sand and gravel, and submerged it in the water. He broke up the dirt-clods and vigorously agitated the material: back and forth, back and forth. The water carried away a cloud of dirt. He lifted the bowl from the river and picked out the pebbles. Then he started moving the bowl in tight circles. Around and around the water swirled, carrying the lighter sand with it. When he tilted the lip of the bowl forward, this material was swept into the river. He refilled the bowl with water and repeated the process, over and over, always keeping his movements smooth and rhythmic. Each time, he lost a little more sand. Finally he was left with a palmful of dark and dense material. At this point, he gently shook the bowl from side to side so that the "black sand" fanned out and settled to the bottom. He invited the three onlookers to take a peek. As K'uchi-Wara looked into the wooden vessel, he saw among the dark particles a shiny yellow lump the size of a prickly pear seed. There also were a few flecks of yellow.

"Is that the *gold*?" he asked Waman, indicating the tiny nugget.

"It sure is."

The boy was disappointed. "But it's so little."

"Yes," his father chimed in. "It seems like a lot of effort for little reward."

"True," responded the priest. "But consider this: every day, from dawn to dusk, we have hundreds of workers line up along this river and pan for the metal. Although each bowlful of gravel yields only a little gold, it all adds up. I think you'd be surprised how much gold this mine produces in a year!"

The Diaguita worker motioned for the mine overseer, who also was Diaguita, to come over. As the overseer approached, he gave Waman,

K'uchi-Wara, and his father a nod. Then he produced a leather pouch from inside his tunic. Untying the string that bound its opening, he carefully reached into the bowl and extracted the tiny nugget. He likewise fished out the gold flecks, all of which were deposited in the pouch.

"What happens to the gold that's found here?" K'uchi-Wara asked the priest.

"It's melted down and formed into ingots. They're sent by llama train to Cuzco."

"And what happens when it reaches Cuzco?"

Waman smiled, being used to the boy's never-ending stream of questions. "Once in the capital, it's divvied up."

"Do the king and his family get some of the gold? I'll bet they *do!*" K'uchi-Wara thought back to the *qhapaq hucha* festival, when he had seen the monarch, the queen, and two of their daughters, all of whom had worn adornments of the metal.

"Of course. And some of it's used to support religious activities."

"Really? What sorts of activities?"

"Well, a lot of gold goes to the royal workshops. There artisans fashion it into statuettes in the form of people and animals. The statuettes are distributed to *waqas* all over the realm, where they're left as offerings. If I'm not mistaken, among the sacrificial materials that you received was a golden llama. It'll be left with you on the summit of Titi-Urqu. Now, how'd you like to try *your* hand at looking for gold?"

As it turned out, the day was not only sunny, but hot. In the afternoon, after a dismal attempt at panning, K'uchi-Wara gave up. He had not found a single fleck of gold. He, his father, and Waman walked downstream from where the Diaguita were still hard at work. When they reached a sand-spit that jutted out into the river, they immediately stripped, dropped their clothing, and plunged into the water. Submerging himself completely, the boy felt cool and refreshed. As he came up for breath, though, he was hit in the face by a wall of water. "What the ...?" he sputtered, as he swallowed some liquid. He then realized that his father was splashing him. He turned his head to the side and shouted,

"OH, YEAH? Two can play at your game!" And he started splashing his father back. When Waman joined the fray, a three-way water-war began. K'uchi-Wara hadn't had so much fun in a long time. For a brief moment, he forgot about the approaching sacrifice.

* * *

Back in the Mapocho Valley, the boy and priest resumed their daily observation of Titi-Urqu. One morning, as they stood together on the platform and looked toward the peak, they saw the first of the sun's rays coming from behind it. As the ruddy light fell on the large dome, the ice began to glow purple and red. "*Achalau!*" said K'uchi-Wara.

Waman announced, "The December solstice is here! It's time to celebrate Qhapaq Raymi."

Vitacura toasts Inti as part of the festival of Qhapaq Raymi.

Chapter Thirteen: Titi-Urqu

Qhapaq Raymi honored Inti. It was celebrated in Cuzco and in the provinces at about the same time. Although the festival at the empire's southern extreme was similar to the one in the capital, it was smaller and less elaborate. It began with the initiation rites for adolescent males. Boys between the ages of twelve and fifteen, the sons of Inka officials and important settlers, took part in various rituals. They also underwent a series of trials to prove themselves worthy of being men. K'uchi-Wara was not among them, though, being too young.

As part of the festival, the Old One presided over the sacrifice of five white llamas. His audience included the eight-year-old and his parents; Vitacura and other bureaucrats; members of the priesthood, among them Waman; high-status Diaguita; and elite Pecunche, including Michimalonko and all four of his wives. The senior priest slit the animals' throats. He ordered a group of young women, who were very beautiful and who wore Inka dresses, to collect the blood. They mixed the warm liquid with maize flour to produce a dough. Then they formed the dough into little cakes, which were heaped on a platter and distributed to the audience. As the boy bit into his morsel, he thought, *Atatau–this tastes awful! Maybe I can spit it out.* But when he looked around, he saw other people finishing theirs, so he choked it down.

When everyone was done, the Old One said to them, "You've just eaten the food of the Sun. It'll remain in your bodies for the entire year, where it'll bear witness to your behavior. If you speak ill of Inti or the king, or if you harbor evil thoughts about them, these things will become known. And — you — will — be — *punished!*"

In the evening, some of the llamas' flesh was thrown into a large bonfire to "nourish" the Sun. The remainder was roasted and served to the audience. The menu also included a vegetable soup that was thickened with *quinua* and flavored with local herbs. K'uchi-Wara ate his fill. He washed the food down with corn-beer, whose taste he had gotten used to, no longer considering it overly sour. He also received coca leaves. All too soon, however, Qhapaq Raymi was over.

A week later, K'uchi-Wara and his parents were relaxing in one of their rooms. His parents had reconciled to the point where they could stand to be in the same place together. All at once, the child felt a slight tremor. "What was that?" he asked his mother.

"What was what?"

"I don't rightly know. For a second, I though the earth was rocking. Wait! There it goes again!"

"Yes, I fee ..."

Before the woman had finished her sentence, the ground was shaking noticeably. What started as a series of nearly imperceptible jerks, changed to a rolling motion. It gradually grew in intensity, and lasted for several "minutes" (each "minute" being the amount of time that a child could hold his breath). At first, the family did not know what to do because they had never experienced an earthquake before. When the walls began to crack, though, the father yelled, "QUICK! Everyone outside!"

As they raced from the building, the cracks widened. The walls began to crumble. No sooner had they reached the safety of the outdoors, than they heard a loud CRASH! The roof had collapsed.

* * *

Vitacura called an afternoon meeting to discuss the implications of the earthquake. The meeting had to take place in the courtyard of his residence. Like many buildings at the administrative center, the residence itself had been badly damaged. The meeting was attended by K'uchi-Wara's parents, the Old One, and Waman.

The five people took their seats on low stools. Vitacura spoke first: "I'm happy to report that nobody was seriously hurt in the tremor. We were fortunate! But we may not be so lucky next time." Turning to the senior priest, he asked, "Why do you think the earth shook so violently?"

The Old One gave a snort. "The answer's straightforward. The mountain-*waqa* grows impatient! He's clamoring for his sacrifice! If we don't acquiesce to his wishes, and soon, he'll take his due by force."

"Your views are clear enough," said the governor. Then he addressed Waman. "What's your opinion?"

Before Waman could speak, however, the senior priest, his posture stiffening, protested, "Why're you asking him? He's just a neophyte. What does he know about deciphering omens? Or about divining the will of the gods?"

"Nonetheless, I'd like to hear what he has to say."

The junior priest squirmed uncomfortably on his stool. "Well, sir," he hemmed and hawed, "I think ... perhaps ... Titi-Urqu's not quite ... that is to say, maybe the *waqa*'s ... um ... unhappy with the sacrifice. Yes, maybe the mountain doesn't like our choice of a victim, which is why he rocked the earth."

Vitacura reacted with a nearly imperceptible nod.

As for K'uchi-Wara's mother, she could not believe her ears. *Maybe my son will be saved! Waman, I could give you a big hug!*

"Absurd!" retorted the Old One, his face turning red.

Hearing this one word, the woman thought, *Oh, I want so badly to slap your face! Or to take this mantle from around my shoulders and stuff it down your throat. Anything to shut you up!* But being the wife of a lowly noble from the provinces, she could say nothing.

The senior priest went on: "Why would the *waqa* reject our sacrifice? *Huh?*" As he spat out the last word, he scowled at the junior priest.

So awful was the expression on the Old One's face, the woman was surprised that Waman didn't instantly turn to stone. Glancing into the junior priest's eyes, she saw the desperation of a hunted animal. He took a deep breath and answered, "Well ... perhaps ... on account of his physical flaws? ... like the warts on his hands or the scar on his knee."

The senior priest was exasperated. "We've revisited this issue time and time again. When the Apu-Panaka selected the boy, he knew all about the imperfections! Yet he considered the child to be the preference of the mountain-*waqas*. And to be satisfactory—despite his blemishes."

"No!" declared Waman, sitting up straight. He seemed to gain confidence as he charged ahead with his words. "The Apu-Panaka said that K'uchi-Wara was loved by the major *waqa* of his *homeland*. Not necessarily by Titi-Urqu. Maybe Titi-Urqu would prefer a local child instead!"

The Old One, his lips pursed, continued to glare at the junior priest. Undeterred, Waman said: "I firmly believe that we should choose a flawless boy from the Mapocho Valley. He'll take K'uchi-Wara's place on the peak. And we can bestow on him all the items originally given to K'uchi-Wara for the sacrifice."

The Old One could contain himself no longer. Turning to Vitacura, he blurted out, "As you know, sir, our relationship with the Pecunche is precarious. I don't think we can risk alienating Michimalonko by immolating one of his own people."

Vitacura sighed. He looked at each participant in turn. "Let me consider what's been said here, and what course of action we should take. I'll tell you what I've decided tomorrow. You can go."

K'uchi-Wara's mother was very agitated that night. Unable to keep still, she paced the floor of the building to which the family had been moved—a building with an intact roof. As she walked back and forth, she silently prayed. *Oh, Father-Sun and Mother-Earth, please don't let the Inkas take my boy! Oh, Titi-Urqu, I beseech you, I IMPLORE YOU, plant a seed of doubt in Vitacura's heart as to my son's worthiness! Do this for me and I promise that I'll weave you ten tunics from the finest alpaca wool! I'll slaughter twenty guinea pigs and five llamas in your name! I'll ... I'll ... throw myself off the platform on Huelén Hill! I OFFER YOU MY LIFE IN*

EXCHANGE FOR MY CHILD'S!

Her husband, seeing how anxious she was, tried to get her to sit down. To no avail. He told her, "I know you're hoping that the governor reverses the decision to offer up our boy. I share your hope! But suppose you let yourself get all worked up and he doesn't save our son—then what? I fear that you'll be completely overwhelmed by your feelings. And you might let your anger or sadness or remorse show. I don't have to remind you that the Inkas forbid us from any outward display of emotion connected with the upcoming event."

The following day, Vitacura called the parents and priests together to notify them of his decision. As she waited for him to speak, the mother was filled with optimism—*please, please, please*—and dread.

"After careful consideration ..." the governor began.

Please, please, please.

"... I have concluded that ..."

Please, please, please.

"... the senior priest is right. The mountain-*waqa* grows impatient. So the child should be sacrificed as soon as possible!"

The woman gasped. She felt like someone had punched her in the gut. She wanted to scream, tear out her hair, kick the walls, die. But she could do nothing.

* * *

The Inkas quickly and efficiently organized an expedition to Titi-Urqu. They dispatched a large group of laborers to the peak. The men were to repair a string of stone huts along the route to and on the slopes of the mountain. They also had to build a structure on the summit plateau where the victim would be buried. Furthermore, as there was no dirt on the peak for filling the structure, they were charged with hauling loads of earth up from the base.

It was decided that the same people who had accompanied K'uchi-Wara on his trip from Cuzco should go with him to Titi-Urqu: his parents, the state official, the Old One, Waman, the attendants, and the llama train drivers. They would take the personal effects of the party, bedding, enough food for a month, supplies and gear, firewood, and most importantly, the sacrificial items. All this material would be hauled to and up the mountain by thirty llamas.

It was early afternoon. The boy and his mother were sitting outside, enjoying the sunshine and each other's company.

She said, "Have I told you how *proud* I am of you?"

"Why? What have *I* done to be proud of?"

"You made a long and difficult journey. And you didn't complain, not even once. Soon you'll be leaving for the house of the gods. I don't think most people could even *imagine* what you've been through, or what you *will be* going through."

"Oh, Mom! You make everything sound so *dramatic*."

"I'm serious! I want you to know that I *love* you. And that I'm proud of you."

* * *

Meanwhile Vitacura and the Old One were meeting in the governor's temporary residence, his new house not having been completed. Once the priest had assured Vitacura that the preparations for the trip to Titi-Urqu had been completed, their conversation turned to other topics. The Old One asked, "Why did you solicit Waman's opinion on the earthquake?"

"I've found that it's often a good idea to get several viewpoints before making up your mind."

"In the end, you made the appropriate decision. As I'm sure you could tell, Waman's judgement was clouded by his affection for the boy."

"No doubt about that."

"So we need to dispatch K'uchi-Wara as quickly as possible."

"I agree." Then, changing the flow of the conversation, Vitacura said, "I'm curious, how do you, as a priest, see the sacrifice of the *qhapaq huchas*?"

The Old One considered for a moment. Then he said, "Envision Tawantin-Suyu as a living organism with Cuzco as the heart. For me, the distribution of children from the capital to the farthest reaches of the empire is analogous to the circulation of blood from the heart to the rest of the body. When the *qhapaq huchas* are offered up, their vitality nourishes the *waqas*. And it animates the land."

"Maybe this isn't a fair question, but do you *really* believe your dogma?"

"Yes, I can say with complete confidence that if we didn't carry out the immolations, then our kingdom would die."

"I agree with you! As part of the royal government, though, I tend to see the *qhapaq huchas* in political terms."

"How so?"

"I believe that we Inkas are a superior people ..."

"Without doubt."

Vitacura continued, "... and one of the most effective ways to show our domination of inferior peoples is to take the children of their rulers for sacrifice. Because when we do that, we instill in our subjects the idea that we have the power of life and death over them, which means they'll be less likely to rebel against us."

A *chaski* burst into the room. He bowed to the governor, and said breathlessly, "I'm sorry to disturb you, sir. I have bad news from Cuzco. The king's come down with a strange illness. It's feared he may die."

The Old One gave Vitacura a grave look. "This makes it even more imperative that we dispatch K'uchi-Wara to Titi-Urqu! Without delay! Because when the *qhapaq hucha* is sacrificed to the *waqa* in the name of the king, then the *waqa* will be obliged to aid the king in his recovery."

"I see," said the governor. "Okay, we'll have a send-off for the boy to-morrow morning." Then, returning his attention to the *chaski*, he asked, "Do you have any more news for us?"

"Yes! Curious rumors have reached the capital from the north coast. The northerners claim to have encountered strange men. Apparently these men arrived on houses that float on water. They're said to be tall, pale, and have hairy faces. They speak gibberish, like the chattering of monkeys. They carry long sticks that produce a deafening sound, like a thunderclap. And the queerest thing of all: we're told that they're obsessed with gold. So much so, it's believed that they eat the metal!"

"You certainly bring strange and sobering news, runner," responded Vitacura. "But tell me, is it known where the alien men came from? And what they want? Also, is there any connection between their arrival and the king's illness?"

The discussion continued late into the evening.

* * *

The mood was somber, the morning chilly, when the child and his entourage left the settlement in the Mapocho Valley. Despite the chill in the air, a crowd of Inkas, Diaguita, and Pecunche turned out to see the *qhapaq hucha* off, and to wish him well. The group headed south. They followed a path that cut through the middle of the forest, which stood dense and dusky. Given that the boy had spent his life in the open terrain above the tree line, walking through the woods made him feel as if the world were closing in on him. It seemed like he were surrounded by an ever deepening darkness. *It's suffocating in here!*

K'uchi-Wara looked straight up and through a gap between the tops of the trees. The sky overhead was filled with grey clouds being pushed along by a restless wind. Whenever the clouds parted, a shaft of sunlight would appear through the gap. It shone down into the forest, penetrating its murk and creating a shimmering patch along the trail. But then the wind would drive the clouds together. And the sunbeam would disappear, together with the flickering patch.

The party walked single file, with the Old One leading. Behind him came K'uchi-Wara. To take his mind off the creepy feeling that the tall trees were giving him, he started watching the little patches of sunshine that materialized in the distance. In his imagination, they seemed to play and dance. Since they helped to dispel the gloom of the woods, they made him feel better. He noticed, though, that every time the priest reached one of them, it appeared to vanish. After seeing this happen several times, the child tugged at the hem of the Old One's mantle.

"Sir ..."

"Yes?" the man replied, neither stopping, nor turning around.

"Why does the light dislike you?"

"Huh? What are you babbling about?"

"It seems like the sunshine's afraid of you! Whenever you get near it, it hides!"

"Oh, hush! You're speaking complete nonsense!"

K'uchi-Wara did as he was told. It dismayed him, though, to think that there were men in the world who were so severe and hard-hearted, they could drive away the daylight.

The group followed the Mapocho River to its junction with the Molina, the Molina River to its confluence with the Cepo, and the Cepo River to its source. They covered the same ground that would be covered by Gerardo and Jaime many centuries later. They noticed that the vegetation changed with the altitude. As they slowly climbed, the trees were supplanted by scrubby plants, which gave way to cacti and thorny bushes, which were replaced by bunchgrasses.

The party slept in the stone huts that had been recently repaired by the gang of workers. Although the structures had no roofs, the attendants had brought wooden poles and large mats of woven *ichu*. They readied each hut by placing the poles across the walls like beams and by pulling a mat over the poles like thatch. The corners of the mat were anchored with rocks. A second mat and woolen blankets were placed on the floor for insulation.

Once the attendants had made the huts livable, they built a fire and prepared dinner. Given the sacredness of the group's mission, however, its members had to fast. The fasting had started when Qhapaq Raymi ended. It meant that they had to abstain from meat, salt, chili peppers, and *chicha*. So their meals typically consisted of potatoes, corn, and vegetables. There being little to do after dinner, K'uchi-Wara usually curled up in a warm blanket and slept.

* * *

One night, the boy dreamt of his homeland. He had not seen it for over six months. He was a condor flying over his community, and spied far below his extended family's homestead with its four cottages, oval gardens, and rectangular corrals. He gazed at the compounds of other families. They were evenly spaced across the mountain slope and connected by footpaths. On the flat area above Wila-Nayra, he saw the pools, including the one called "Red-Eye." At the top of the ridge, he identified the burial towers where his ancestors had been laid to rest. Continuing his aerial journey, the child-condor came upon a lone figure standing in a pasture, watching his flock. As he approached, he was overjoyed to see that it was Jukumari. He came face to face with his cousin. Suddenly the latter transformed into a *qhapaq hucha*. Not just any *qhapaq hucha*, but the one who had appeared in his nightmare at the base of Putina Volcano.

"I'll see you soon," the dead boy said. K'uchi-Wara looked into his sunken eyes and screamed.

* * *

K'uchi-Wara was sullen in the morning. His father had noticed that he was becoming increasingly tense, had heard him shout in terror during the night, and knew exactly what was wrong. Nonetheless he wanted his son to open up about his feelings; thus he asked, "What's the matter?"

"Well," the child replied. "I don't want to be a *qhapaq hucha* anymore. It was fun for a while. Now I just want to go home."

"Unfortunately ... we can't go home," the man said very softly.

"*P-l-e-a-s-e?!*"

The father looked into his boy's eyes. He noted that they were welling with tears. He saw desperation there too, which had not been there before. *I feel every bit as impotent as your mother has accused me of being!* He hugged the child, held him in his arms for a long time. He said, "No

... we can't go home ... but it's going to be *okay*." Then he repeated the speech that the Inkas had given him many times. He periodically recited it to convince himself of its truth. "Son," he began, "I know you're afraid to meet and serve the *waqa*! You shouldn't be, though. Because you're going to a *wonderful* place. It's a place where you'll always be *happy*. Where you'll want for nothing. Where you'll never get sick or grow old. Doesn't that sound *great*? So give me a smile, won't you?"

"But I—I'm *scared*."

"I know you are. That's only natural! Do you want to know what I do when I'm frightened?"

"You? You get scared?"

"Of course, I do! And when I'm afraid, I repeat the words to a song that my father taught me. It goes like this:

'I am the sunlight
That shines on a peak,
While fear is the wind
That roars about me.
No matter its force
It cannot touch me!
So let the wind howl
It will not stop me!'

Now, you say the words back to me."

* * *

A week after leaving the Inka settlement, the group reached what would come to be called the "Numbered Rock." It was a boxcar-sized boulder that in the future would shelter Gerardo and Jaime. There they set up camp. In the evening, having supped, K'uchi-Wara sat at the foot of the boulder, under an overhang of rock. He gazed up at Titi-Urqu's massive dome. It was glorious! During their departure from the Mapocho Valley, when the sky had been partly overcast, the mountain had received a dusting of white. With the sun making its descent, the snow glowed with brilliant color. It changed from scarlet to crimson to magenta to purple, as the reds became deeper and the blues more pronounced. As the light continued to fade, the peak turned to violet. Then the alpenglow was gone, forms became indistinct and dusky, and the blackness of a moonless night descended.

The next day, the boy and his entourage walked from the Numbered Rock to the foot of Titi-Urqu. As they slowly ascended the valley, its floor became narrower and more rugged. The rock walls on either side rose higher and grew more precipitous. The bunchgrasses that thrived around the boulder were supplanted by cushion plants, which were themselves replaced by mosses and lichens. The more they climbed, the thinner the air became. And the harder it was to breath.

The party spent several days at their next camp. It consisted of seven huts situated in a large basin. Nearby was a stream that gushed from a pool that was fed by runoff from a glacier that flowed down Titi-Urqu's face. The glacier, a tongue of greenish-blue ice, was warped and fractured. Frozen turrets projected from it.

The Old One decided to stay at this spot not only so everyone could get used to the altitude, but so he could carry out some preparatory rites associated with the sacrifice. To that end, he and Waman got together with K'uchi-Wara and his mother. As they stood outside under an azure sky, the senior priest said, "In anticipation of the boy being united with the *waqa*, he must be purified and sanctified. The first step to purification is confession. That's why we're here. We'll bear witness to the child's recitation of sins."

"*Sins?*" K'uchi-Wara's mother blurted out. "Are you kidding? He's only eight years old! No, he just had his birthday, so he's nine. Even so, what would a boy his age have to confess?"

"There's thievery, witchcraft, failure to show a *waqa* the proper respect ..."

"Really, if that isn't the most *ridiculous!*" the woman interrupted.

"K'uchi-Wara," the Old One continued, "this is a matter of great importance, regardless of what your mother thinks! Have you ever been disrespectful of the king? Or *blasphemed* against Inti?"

"What does b-l-a-s-p-h-e-m-e-d mean?" the child asked.

"I'm getting too old for this job," the elderly priest muttered under his breath. "I'm tired of dealing with children and their provincial parents. I can't wait to return to Cuzco." Then he said aloud, "Here's what we're going to do! We'll have you perform a ritual ablution. That'll rid you of your sins."

The Old One led Waman, the boy, and his mother from their camp to the little pool. They followed the stream up a gentle slope. As he walked, K'uchi-Wara listened to the clack, clack, clack of rock against rock under his bare feet.

When they reached the edge of the pool, the senior priest faced the child. "Now you must strip and immerse yourself in the sacred waters. In this way, you'll be purified. And you'll become worthy to be received by the mountain-*waqa*."

K'uchi-Wara looked at the tranquil pool. A thin ribbon of ice had formed along its border. Ice also circled the rocks that poked above the water. He reached down, dipping his fingers in the pool. "*ALALAU!*" he exclaimed. "That's *frigid!*"

"What do you expect? It's runoff from a glacier," said the Old One.

"I *can't* go in there. I'll *freeze* to death! Besides, I *hate* taking baths."

"Is this *really* necessary?" asked the mother. "It seems excessive to me."

"Yes, it's *absolutely* necessary," replied the senior priest, annoyed.

Waman intervened. "Look, K'uchi-Wara, I know that you're going to get a *real* shock when you get in the water. But as you enter, think of pleasant things. Imagine that you're back at the Marga-Marga Mine. It's a hot sticky day, and you're going for a refreshing dip in the river. Think you can do that?"

The child nodded.

"Good boy."

"Okay," said the Old One, "let's get this over with."

K'uchi-Wara removed his mantle, handing it to his mother. Then he pulled his tunic off over his head and gave it to her. He reluctantly stepped toward the pool. At Waman's urging, he plunged right in. The cold stunned him. It rendered him incapable of thought. The two priests invoked the gods and started chanting a prayer. When the child stumbled from the water a short time later, he was hunched over like an old man, and was hugging himself as if for dear life. His penis had shrunk to almost nothing, his lips had turned blue, and his teeth were chattering uncontrollably. Waman immediately wrapped him in a large woolen blanket.

* * *

Once K'uchi-Wara had had a chance to warm up and get dressed, his mother took him by the hand and led him away from the others. She sat him down on a rock and said, "I'm going to fix your hair. I want you to look your *best* when you meet the *waqa*. As a *qhapaq hucha*, you'll be representing our province. So I thought that I'd braid your hair in a traditional Lupaka style. That way, everyone—even the gods—will know who you are and where you're from." She produced a wooden comb from the bag that she carried and started running it through his long locks. It took her a while to disentangle them. She pulled out a jar containing oil, which she rubbed into his hair to make it smooth and shiny. Then she spent an hour—the time it took her to boil a pot of potatoes—meticulously weaving his tresses into hundreds of plaits. "There! You look very *handsome*. Come here and give your mother a hug."

As she held the boy, an unwelcome thought intruded. *He's supposed to be offered up in a few days. Just a few days. Then he'll be lost to me forever!* Reflecting on the magnitude of her loss, she held her son tighter. Tears streamed down her face. She started to sob, her body to convulse. "Those ... those ... *bastards!* What right do they have to take you from me? What did you ever *do - to - them*?" She spat out the last words.

"Mama! Are you okay?"

"I'm ... I'm sorry.... Yes, I'm fine."

She released the child. Doing so, she realized that he had been putting up a brave front for her. She had to do the same for him. *He's been having a tough time dealing with all this. I don't need to make it harder for him by going to pieces. I'll be cool and composed for the next few days. Only when this is all over, and I'm as far from the Inkas as I can get, will I grieve for him. Then for the rest of my life, I'll honor him by preparing his favorite foods. And by feeding his spirit.*

* * *

That evening, K'uchi-Wara's father felt a desperate need to be alone. Leaving the huts behind, he followed the stream to the pool where his son had taken his ritual bath. He stopped briefly to gaze across it. Then he continued on his way, walking upslope on glacial till. He soon reached a maze of jumbled ice towers. Wandering through it, always ascending, he finally came to an open space with a view toward Titi-Urqu's glaciated face. He reached down and grabbed a rock. Looking up, he hurled the rock with all his strength toward the peak. At the same time, he yelled as loudly as he could, "CURSE YOU, *WAQA*! I've lost my wife because of you. Soon I'll lose my child! You've already taken my dignity, you might as well take my life! Why not knock over an ice tower and crush me! What've I got to live for!" He raged against the mountain until he was exhausted. As night came on, with head down, he trudged back to camp.

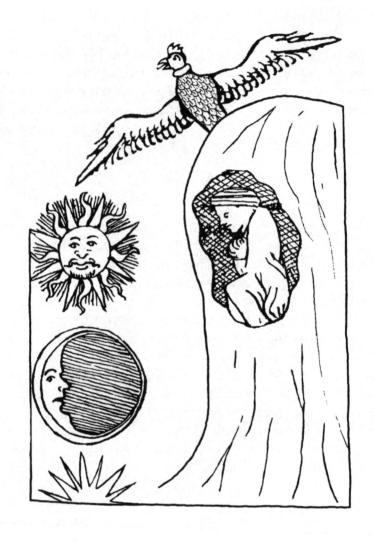

Child entombed within Titi-Urqu (circa 1500)

Chapter Fourteen: The Sacrifice

It was night. The wind was howling outside the stone structure where K'uchi-Wara and his parents were trying to sleep. Their small hut, one of several, was located high on Titi-Urqu's main ridge. The boy's inability to sleep was due not only to the roar of the storm and the crowded conditions in the shelter, but to the altitude. He had a headache and nausea. Also he was worried about the upcoming sacrifice. It was scheduled to take place in two days, weather permitting.

The child and his entourage had climbed to the uppermost camp the previous day. Leaving the huts in the basin at dawn, they had made their way up a scree-covered secondary ridge to the peak's face. Where the ridge joined the face, the slope became very steep, and the going difficult. As the boy had trouble walking, he had to be helped by his father and Waman. He became bone-weary, and had to stop many times to catch his breath. "*Ananau!*" he panted. "How tiring!" Higher still, the group reached a "road" built by the laborers who had been sent by the Inkas. The road was paved with flat stones. It was marked every so often with rock cairns. Following it, they zigzagged up the side of the mountain. They eventually arrived at the main ridge, and shortly thereafter at the huts.

Although the wind died down in the morning, the weather remained foul, threatening snow. K'uchi-Wara and his parents mostly stayed in the shelter, trying to keep warm. Once when the child went out to pee, his exposed flesh began to freeze. So he hurried back inside.

Later that day, he checked the cloth bag he always carried. He wanted to make sure his sling was inside. To his dismay, it was gone! "Dad," he called out, "have you seen my *sling*?"

"No, son. The last time I remember seeing it was ... let me think ... when you were playing with it by the large boulder."

"That was ages ago! Mom, do *you* know where my sling is?"

"No, dear. Have you looked inside your bag?"

"Of course! That's the first place I checked."

"How about inside the llama-sack that holds our personal effects."

K'uchi-Wara rummaged around in the large bag, searching for his sling. When he did not find it, he became frantic. He started pulling out items as fast as he could and throwing them around the hut.

"Hey, hey," his father said, trying to calm him. He crawled over to the boy, the only type of movement possible in their cramped quarters, and hugged him. "It's okay, it's okay. I'll help you look for your sling." Try as they might, though, they could not find it. The child was heartbroken.

On Titi-Urqu's summit, the gang of workers had finished building the structure where K'uchi-Wara was to be entombed. They were in the process of transporting the last loads of dirt from the base of the peak. As instructed, they would top off the structure with soil. But they would leave a hole in the middle of it, and a pile of soil nearby to fill the hole.

Meanwhile the Inka priests carried out more preparatory rites. They squeezed into the hut with K'uchi-Wara and his parents, holding small pots. The pots contained pigments. While the Old One recited prayers, Waman took a dab of red paint and smeared it over the child's face. As the incantations continued, yellow lines were added. The junior priest applied four stripes to each side of the boy's head. "That should do it," he said, admiring his handiwork.

"Now we have to induce you to break your fast," the Old One told K'uchi-Wara. "When you encounter the mountain-*waqa*, you must be satiated and content. I'll have the attendants prepare a generous meal for you."

"But sir," the child protested, "I can't eat! My stomach's upset, and I feel nauseous."

"Those are typical symptoms of *suruchi*, altitude sickness. What you need is a coca-leaf tea."

Once the boy had drunk the warm liquid, he felt somewhat better. The father insisted on serving him his last meal. He brought one dish after another into the hut: roasted llama meat, corn gruel, cooked vegetables, and boiled potatoes, all seasoned with salt. At his urging, K'uchi-Wara forced a little food down.

It was the child's last night. Terrified of what would be taking place the next day, he could not sleep. Instead he quietly repeated, over and over as if it were a mantra, the words to his father's song. "I am the sunlight that shines on a peak, while fear is the wind...."

His mother heard his mumbling and sensed his restlessness. She tried to comfort and quiet him. "Come snuggle up with me," she whispered, lifting her blanket so he could crawl underneath it. She cradled him.

It seemed to take forever for morning to arrive; it arrived all too soon. The state official did not have to leave his hut to wake the boy and his parents. They had barely closed their eyes during the night. They got up and dressed. K'uchi-Wara, who was already wearing his tunic, donned the moccasins, silver bracelet, headband, pendant, and headdress. Then he wrapped his mantle about his body. Pushing aside the woven flap that covered the entrance to the structure, he stepped outside.

The cold was intense! It took his breath away. It burned any exposed flesh. Although the landscape was still shrouded in darkness and overhead he could see stars, the boy knew that dawn was not far off. There was a faint glow toward the east. His mother and father, the official, the Old One, Waman, and the attendants joined him in the open air.

Just upslope from the huts was the temple that Gerardo and Jaime would stumble onto almost half a millennium later. The victim and other participants in the ceremony stood on this circular platform. They faced east. Looking from one person to the next, the child saw that they were elegantly dressed, especially the official and priests. The former wore a brilliantly colored feather cape and an assortment of gold adornments. The adornments included bracelets, ear-spools, and a pectoral. The latter had donned brightly hued tunics, headdresses made from the plumes of Amazonian birds, gold and silver ornaments.

There was a flash on the horizon. The solar disk began its ascent. The priests paid homage to their principal god by bowing to him and by raising their arms with the palms toward him. They made a kissing sound with their mouths, touched their fingers to their lips, and offered a prayer.

An attendant lit a small fire next to the platform. Because of the rarified atmosphere, he had considerable difficulty. He stuck some pieces of wood into it that burned with a fragrant smell. Another attendant, holding a small drum, took up a slow beat. And the third, grasping a trumpet fashioned from a conch shell, blew a long mournful note. Meanwhile Waman chanted.

Reminiscent of the rites performed in Cuzco, the Old One led K'uchi-Wara twice around the circular temple, while giving the following oration:

"Oh, Inti, who gives us night and day, preserve the lord Inka. Grant that he may be victorious over his enemies, and that he may always be a conqueror. Give him peace and prosperity. Keep him safe from harm.

"Oh, mountain-god, who gives us water, multiply the fruits of the earth so your people don't suffer from hunger. Make the corn grow tall and strong and plentiful. Multiply the flocks. Let them bring forth young.

"Oh, mighty *waqa*, father of the Pecunche, we offer you this *qhapaq hucha* in the name of Wayna Qhapaq, that you might look kindly on the Inkas!"

Waman fetched several bottles containing *chicha*, along with a bag of coca leaves. They had been brought up the peak by a llama. He unstoppered one of the vessels, passing it to the senior priest. The Old One, upon receiving it, noticed that a thin layer of ice was forming in its narrow neck. He broke the ice with his little finger. Turning toward the east and toasting the rising sun, he took a swallow of corn-beer.

Then he poured some of the liquid onto the ground as a libation for Inti. He honored the mountain-*waqa* too, taking a draught himself before draining some *chicha* for the deity. The process was repeated with K'uchi-Wara offering toasts to the Sun and to Titi-Urqu. The Old One made the boy take several deep swallows of the brew. It was cold, thick, and strong. The other players in the drama drank as well, going in order of their status.

The senior priest opened the bag of coca he was handed and selected three perfect leaves. He also accepted a gourd containing lime. He sprinkled some of the powder onto the leaves, rolled them up, and stuck them in his mouth. He slowly masticated them. As with the corn-beer, he offered coca to Inti and the mountain-*waqa*. Their share was burned in the ritual fire. Then the Old One chose a handful of flawless leaves for K'uchi-Wara, a portion of which the child chewed. The rest were for the gods. When he had finished, the other participants partook of the coca.

The boy's mind was getting hazy. The combination of alcohol and coca he had ingested was having an effect, greatly magnified by the altitude. He experienced a confused jumble of sensations. There was the bitter taste of the leaves in his mouth; the aroma of incense from the burning wood; the flash of sunlight reflecting off the metal adornments; the sound of the drum, horn, and human voices; the intense cold that cut to the bone; and the sight of brightly colored figures moving around and around the circular platform. He felt dizzy. He was swooning. He vomited down the front of his tunic.

As the first part of the sacrificial rite ended, so did the involvement of half the participants. The second and more sacred part, the setting for which would be the structure on the summit, would involve only the priests, the official, and the *qhapaq hucha*. The child said goodbye to his parents. It was a somber parting. He hugged each one. His mother, true to her word that she would put on a brave face for her son, did not cry. Nor did she hold him for too long as they embraced for the last time.

The sacrificial party walked from the platform to the end of the spit of broken rock that stuck out into the glacier. From there they had to ascend the steep slope of snow and ice. Staring at the slope, K'uchi-Wara was dazzled by the radiance of the sunlight that reflected from it. And he was awed by the color of the sky above it: dark blue, like lapis lazuli, grading almost to black. Before stepping onto the ice, he turned for a last look at his parents. He waved to them; they waved back.

Getting up the mountain's icy flank proved to be difficult. The boy tried wearing his moccasins, but found that the soles were too smooth and did not get any traction on the snow. So he went barefoot. Walking without shoes did not bother him, though, since he had never used them during his life. Waman took the lead. He held a staff in his hand that he used to steady himself while he kicked steps into the packed snow. His was no easy task, considering he wore only wool socks and flimsy sandals. K'uchi-Wara was right behind the young priest, followed by the official, and the Old One. The latter two also carried walking-sticks.

The child found that if he stamped his foot into a just-made step, his toes could grip the compacted snow and he would not slip. At least he would not slip much. It was hard work. Over time he grew wearier and wearier, which meant he had to stop more often to rest. He also became clumsier and increasingly indifferent to his situation. He started slipping and falling. Luckily the two men behind him were able to catch him before he went careening down the slope. The day wore on. The boy's feet, especially the right one, began to swell from the abuse they were taking. And his hands, try as he might to keep them warm by wrapping them in his mantle, were freezing. He could no longer feel them. Four of the fingers on his left hand were turning bluish-black, a clear sign of frostbite. K'uchi-Wara felt sick and demoralized. *If the Old One wants me to get to the top of this mountain, he can carry me up.* Then he noticed that the gradient was easing, and that the ice and snow were thinning out. He had reached his destination.

The child flopped down and rested with his back against the stone structure. He was exhausted. His heart was hammering in his chest, and he was panting. The three men took seats on large rocks because they too were tired. After a while, Waman got up to look around. The laborers had built the structure on a large plateau near the base of a rocky pyramid. The pyramid was visible from the Mapocho Valley as the mountain's "nipple."

Waman called to the boy. "Hey, K'uchi-Wara, come over here! I want to show you something."

The child stood up too quickly. As the blood rushed from his head, he almost fainted. He put his hand against the structure to steady himself. Recovering somewhat—he was still groggy from the coca, *chicha*, and his exertions—he stumbled over to Waman. As he reached the junior priest, the latter turned toward the north. Waman extended his arm and swept it in a great arc that took in the most amazing panorama the boy had ever seen.

"This will be your domain from now on," declared the priest, a smile on his lips.

K'uchi-Wara looked out into the boundless space. The air was clear, the sky cloudless. Stretching from Titi-Urqu to the horizon, he could see one snow-capped peak after another. *I feel like a condor flying high over the earth and peering down on all creation.* The sound of Waman's voice brought him back to *terra firma*.

The priest was indicating a hulk of a mountain that towered over everything around it. He said, "That's Aconcagua, the *waqa* Qispi serves. The two of you will be able to see one another, and to keep in touch." Waman put his hand on the child's shoulder and gently turned him toward the west. He pointed toward a thin blue line beyond a distant range of rugged hills. "That's the ocean. You once told me that more than anything, you wanted to see Mama-Qucha. Well, there she is! She's part of your grand vista." Then the priest drew his attention to a valley in the middle distance. "That's the Mapocho. From your aerie up here, you'll look down on the Inkas and the Pecunche. And from now till eternity, people will climb to the top of Huelén Hill, where they'll gaze up at *you*."

The Old One called to them. "Let's commence with the ceremony!" They returned to the stone structure, K'uchi-Wara hobbling. As they reached the senior priest, he looked at the child and asked, "Are you ready?"

"Um ... I have to pee." The boy pulled up his tunic and urinated. The liquid hit a rock and spattered. It froze instantly, forming citrine crystals that sparkled in the sunlight.

Waman gathered together the sacrificial offerings and three wooden shovels. They had been brought to the site the previous day by the workers. For his part, the official lifted K'uchi-Wara and set him on top of the structure's rock wall. He pulled the child's moccasins from a cloth bag. He tried to gently place them on the child's feet, but the feet were so badly swollen, the shoes didn't fit. He finally had to yank them on. Then the official hoisted the boy from the wall and lowered him into the hole in the middle of the structure.

As there was little room at the bottom of the cavity, K'uchi-Wara had to curl up in a fetal position. When his buttocks touched the floor, they immediately began to burn. The hole had been dug into the frozen slope. It was deathly cold. He scanned the wall of soil just inches from his head. There were large ice crystals in it. He crossed his legs, pulled his black tunic over his knees and as far down his legs as possible, and wrapped his grey mantle around his body. His efforts at keeping warm were in vain. The boy could hear men's voices coming from above. He had little interest in what they were saying, though.

Waman got down on his belly and sidled over to the hole. He poked his head and shoulders into the cavity. The Old One handed him the offerings. He reached down and carefully set them beside K'uchi-Wara. There was a bag covered with feathers and full of coca leaves. There also was a leather pouch that contained not only locks of hair and nail clippings from the boy's First Haircutting, but his baby teeth. Waman adjusted the braids, band, and headdress on the *qhapaq hucha's* head. Then he thrust a sling, the child's cherished sling, into his hand. Doing so, he said, "I've been meaning to return this to you. I found it on the trail the other day. You must've dropped it. Use it well in the next world!"

K'uchi-Wara gave him a weak smile. He felt numb. He was terrified. He clenched the sling in his left fist. He wrapped his arms around his knees, closed his eyes, and recited his mantra: *I am the sunlight that shines on a peak, while fear is the wind that roars about me....*

The Old One chanted, "Oh, Titi-Urqu, the most powerful *waqa* in the south, accept our sacrifice of a *qhapaq hucha*. And hear our pleas for help."

... No matter its force, it cannot touch me....

"Oh, merciful mountain, father of the Pecunche, cure Wayna Qhapaq of the disease that afflicts him. Restore him to health and vigor. Do not cut his days short."

... So let the wind howl, it will not stop me....

"Oh, wondrous *waqa*, source of life and strength, keep our kingdom safe from invaders. If the pale men from across the sea prove to be hostile, let us drive them from our lands. Preserve Tawantin-Suyu now and forever."

Finishing his prayer, the senior priest gave the others a nod, whereupon they grabbed the shovels. They began filling the hole with dirt from the nearby pile. First the offerings were covered. Then the *qhapaq hucha*'s moccasins disappeared, followed by his legs, tunic, hands, sling, and mantle.

"Bye K'uchi-Wara," Waman said. "I wish you well."

As the boy rested his head on his breast, it vanished under the rising flood of earth, as did his braids and headdress.

... I am ...

Last to be swallowed up were the black and white condor feathers.

* * *

Above the child's body, the priests interred the pair of llama figurines, the one of gold, the other of shell.

When the three men had finished filling the cavity, they gathered their things and started down the icy slope to the circular temple. If possible, they wanted to make it all the way to the base of the mountain before nightfall.

Epilogue

The date was May 23, 1550. Pedro, accompanied by his Quechua-speaking interpreter, approached a hut in one of the poorer neighborhoods of Cuzco. The city sat in a bowl-shaped valley, along whose rim lived many destitute people. The two men had spent the morning looking for this particular house. In their search, they had trudged up and down countless dirt paths, crisscrossing the upper part of the valley. They had asked innumerable peasants for directions to the home of "Juan, the Inka." At last they had found it.

Pedro glanced at the sky. Although it was overcast, he knew from experience that it would not rain, not at this time of year. He drew his light cloak about his shoulders, and walked up to the hut. Like the other buildings in the area, it was small and decrepit. The mud used to plaster the outer walls was crumbling, exposing the field-stones within. The young man knocked at the door, which consisted of scraps of lumber nailed together. He heard coughing inside. Then a weak voice demanded in Quechua, "Who's there?"

He replied haltingly in the same language, "My name Pedro ... Pedro Cieza de León. I am Spanish." Then, signaling to the man beside him to translate, he said in Spanish, "I'm the official chronicler for the Viceroyalty of Peru. I'd like to speak to you." As Quechua did not have an exact gloss for "chonicler," the interpreter used the Spanish word *cronista*.

"'Chronicler'? What's that?" came the gruff response.

"I record information relating to you Indians. For the Crown. I am ... let's see ... I am to the Spanish what the Khipu-kamayuq was to the

Inkas. Does that make sense?"

"Yes."

"May I come in?"

The rickety door was opened by a frail old man. He was badly stooped, but tried to straighten his back, so that Pedro was able to see his face. It was brown and weathered. His hair was close-cropped and white, his eyes rheumy and clouded. *He's almost blind.*

The old man bid Pedro and his interpreter to enter. Then, taking the one chair in the room, he motioned for his guests to have a seat. The only other piece of furniture, though, was a battered wooden bed, which wobbled as they perched themselves on the edge of it.

"Now," began the old man as he faced them, "what do you want to talk about?"

"Your life before the arrival of the Spanish," replied Pedro through the interpreter. "You see, I've been charged with collecting as much information as possible on life under the Inkas. I'm interested in their history, government, and religion. To that end, I've interviewed many of the Inka nobles who still live in Cuzco. Just the other day, I had a long conversation with a man named Pisca. He was one of King Wayna Qhapaq's captains."

The old man said through the interpreter, "I'm familiar with Pisca. And I've heard about you. Friends report that you're fair in your dealings with native people—that *you* can be trusted."

"Yes."

"Too bad the same can't be said for the *rest* of your people. For the last twenty years, you Spaniards have been taking our lands, abusing our women, overworking our men. But I doubt that you want to discuss *these* things." Then he added in a more relaxed tone, "So you're genuinely interested in the Inka past?"

"Yes, I am."

"What would you like to know?"

"I've been told that you were once a priest. Is that true?"

"Yes," replied the old man. "In my younger years, before I was baptized and given the Christian name 'Juan,' I was an Inka priest. I served Inti, the Sun, and the *waqas*. You know about the *waqas*, don't you? They were the local gods. In those days, I was called 'Waman.'"

"How did you like being an Inka priest?"

"At first it was good. I had status, and the people respected me. I enjoyed all the ritual and pageantry of my position. I especially liked celebrating Qhapaq Raymi. But then I had a horrible experience. It soured me on the priesthood."

"Really? What happened?"

"I don't like to talk about it," said Juan. "It makes me angry and sad. Even so, I will tell you ..." His words were interrupted by a bout of coughing. When it ended, he continued: "I was assigned to escort a boy and his parents from Cuzco to central Chile."

"So? What's so terrible about that?"

"Let me finish. The boy had been designated as a *qhapaq hucha*. Do you understand what that means?"

"No, please explain."

"It means that he was to be sacrificed. To a *waqa*! The *waqa* was located in the extreme south. Our journey there took many months. During that time, I was able to get acquainted with the boy. And the more I got to know him, the more I liked him. Like many children his age— he was about ten—he could be a pain. But he also could be warm and funny. Sometimes his behavior was totally immature. At other times, he seemed wise beyond his years."

"What was his name?"

"Um ... how strange ... I don't remember anymore. It was a long Lupaka name. Now where was I?"

"You were telling me about the child. And about the trip you took with him."

"Right. We escorted him south, to the place you Spaniards call Santiago de la Nueva Extremadura. There we waited—waited for the right time to take him to the mountain. You see, he was to be offered up to a powerful mountain-*waqa*. While we were waiting, there was an earthquake. I should tell you that by then I'd come to believe it was wrong for us to put the boy to death. And I interpreted the earthquake as a sign—a sign that the mountain was unhappy with our choice of a victim. I proposed that we sacrifice someone else in his place."

"What happened?"

"I was overruled by the senior priest. He had no misgivings about offering up the boy. The bastard!"

"How was it carried out?"

"The whole thing was very simple. We took the child to the top of the mountain. We drugged him with *chicha* and coca. Then we buried him alive."

"What was the point of the sacrifice?"

"Good question," said Juan. "To be fair, the senior priest truly believed that it was necessary to carry out. He thought it would end a drought in central Chile—a drought that was ruining the corn crop of the Pecunche. They're the native people there. It also was supposed to restore Wayna Qhapaq's health. The king had come down with a strange illness—an illness never before seen in these lands. And he was dying. At the state level, the sacrifice was meant to preserve our country."

"Do you think it was worth it?"

The old man gave a deep sigh. He looked directly into Pedro's face with his cloudy eyes. "Well, the drought *did* end. But the king died. And Tawantin-Suyu was eventually conquered by your people. So you tell me—*was* it worth it?"

"What happened afterwards?"

"After the sacrifice? I came back to Cuzco with the boy's parents. From here they returned to their homeland. I never saw them again. But I believe that when their son died, so did their love for each other.

"As for the senior priest, he got what he deserved." Juan began to chuckle to himself as he uttered these words. The chuckle, however, turned to a slight cough, which grew to a hacking fit that convulsed his whole body. When the coughing finally subsided, the old man wiped his eyes. "Sorry," he rasped, "I'm not well. And now I've forgotten what

I was going to say. Oh yes, the senior priest received the fate that he deserved. After burying the child alive on the peak, we descended. Our route took us down a steep section of glacier. It was icy and treacherous. The old guy was tired. He kept slipping. At one point, he took a misstep and went sliding downhill. If he'd gone straight down the slope, eventually he'd have stopped. He'd have been badly shaken, but okay. Instead he slid to the right—toward a cliff. The last I saw of him, he went flying over the edge. I'll never forget the look of terror on his face. So you see, I was right after all. The mountain-*waqa* didn't like our sacrifice of the Lupaka boy. Demanding his due, he took the life of the senior priest.

"After I returned to Cuzco, I began to mull over my role in the affair. The more I thought about it, the more disgusted I became. I dropped out of the priesthood. I became bitter. During the Spanish Conquest, I came to believe that our gods had abandoned us. So I converted to Christianity. And I took the name 'Juan.'

"Not a day's gone by that I haven't thought about the child. I've often wondered what would've become of him if he'd been allowed to live. Would he have grown up to become a good man? Would he have married the girl he left behind in his village? How many children would they have had? Would they have been happy? It was my understanding that he'd have succeeded his father as headman. Would he have made a strong leader? It's pointless to dwell on such things, though. It'll drive you crazy.

"Sitting here now, what I remember most about the boy is his courage. He spent over half a year—*half a year*—facing his own demise. But, people have argued, that doesn't mean he was brave; all of us, they say, live with the understanding that sometime we're going to leave this world. And few of us are brave. For most of us, though, the hour of our passing's unknown. So we don't worry about it. But consider the child. As his death was preordained, it had to have been constantly on his mind. And it must've been hard for him to endure—day in and day out—not only the certainty of his death, but the fact that it was getting ever closer. Yes, living under those circumstances was heroic. I believe that in his last six months he showed more courage than I've shown my whole time on this earth. And I've been here for many years."

Then tears began to roll down the old man's weathered face. His voice quavered as he said, "I myself don't have much time left. I pray that when I die, I'll go to heaven. There I hope to see the boy again. I want to tell him that I'm sorry—sorry for what happened to him. He was never baptized. Do you think he got into heaven?"

Pedro looked down at the floor. "I don't really know. I'm not a priest."

* * *

As individuals, we're here only briefly, and all too soon are gone. The human race, however, endures. The descendants of the Lupaka still live around Lake Titicaca, where they grow up, raise families, and breed alpacas. Their children continue to pasture the herds on grassy slopes in the shadow of ice-clad giants.

To this day, the inhabitants of Santiago remember the story of how Gerardo and Jaime made their spectacular find. They still climb to the top of Huelén Hill, which is now a park called Santa Lucía, that is graced with gardens and fountains. They continue to look out over the vast Mapocho Valley—where almost seven million people, most of whom are of mixed Spanish and indigenous blood, live—to the monumental dome in the distance. They are always struck by the peak's grandeur, by its permanent crown of white. And sometimes they wonder about the boy— though his name, K'uchi-Wara, has been forgotten—who five hundred years ago was entombed by the Inkas near its summit. A child of the snows.

Foreign Terms

- **alpaca** (Quechua): domesticated member of the camel family native to the Andes; it was raised for its wool.

- **Apu-Panaka** (Quechua): state official whose job it was to choose children for sacrifice.

- **Atacama**: driest desert on earth; it is located in northern Chile.

- **Awqay-Pata** (Quechua): main plaza in Cuzco.

- **Aymara**: language spoken by the Lupaka and other ethnic groups who lived around Lake Titicaca.

- **ch'arkhi** (Quechua): freeze-dried llama or alpaca meat.

- **chaski** (Quechua): relay runner who carried messages along the royal roads.

- **chicha**: corn beer.

- **Chinchay-Suyu** (Quechua): northwestern quarter of the Inka Empire.

- **chullpa** (Quechua): burial tower.

- **ch'unpi** (Quechua): brown.

- **chuño** (Quechua): freeze-dried potatoes.

- **ch'uspa** (Quechua): small cloth bag used to carry coca leaves.

- **coca** (or "kuka" in Quechua): cultivated plant in western South America whose leaves are chewed as a stimulant.

- **Cuzco** (Quechua): capital of the Inka Empire.

- **Diaguita**: ethnic group from around the Copiapó Valley of Chile.

- **guano** (Quechua): manure from sea birds; it is used for fertilizer.

- **ichu** (Quechua): tough bunchgrass native to the Andes; it was used for feed and thatch.

- **illa** (Quechua): small stone figure of a llama or alpaca; it was believed to be responsible for the fertility of the type of animal it represented.

- **Inka** (Quechua): ethnic group from the highlands of southern Peru who established a vast state.

- **Inti** (Quechua): Sun; patron god of the Inka Empire.

- **kallanka** (Quechua): long hall used by the Inkas to accommodate large numbers of people.

- **k'apa** (Quechua): unit of length equal to a span; distance across an outstretched hand, from the tip of the thumb to the tip of the little finger, or about 9 inches.

- **khipu** (Quechua): Andean recording device consisting of strings in which information was encoded as knots.

- **Khipu-kamayuq** (Quechua): state official who recorded information on knotted strings.

- **khunu-titi** ("snow-cat" in Aymara): white puma killed by K'uchi-Wara.

- **kuraka** (Quechua): local ruler.

- **llama** (Quechua): domesticated member of the camel family native to the Andes; it was raised for meat and as a beast of burden.

- **Lupaka** (Aymara): K'uchi-Wara's ethnic group; they lived on the high plateau around Lake Titicaca.

- **Mama-Killa** (Mother Moon in Quechua): an important Inka goddess; the wife and sister of Inti.

- **Mama-Qucha** (Mother Sea in Quechua; in Aymara, the name is Mama-Kuta): an important Inka goddess.

- **mit'a** (Quechua): labor tax that most subjects of the Inkas owed to the state.

- **mitmaq-kuna** (Quechua): settlers transplanted from one region to another.

- **muru** (Quechua): bald.

- **Pacha-Kuti** ("transformer of the world" in Quechua): Inka king who reigned before K'uchi Wara's time; he conquered the Lupaka.

- **Pecunche**: ethnic group from the Aconcagua and Mapocho Valleys of central Chile.

- **Plomo**, Cerro El ("lead mountain" in Spanish): sacred peak near whose summit a boy was sacrificed.

- **puma** (Quechua): mountain lion native to the Andes.

- **Qala-Uta** ("stone-house" in Aymara): sacred mountain worshipped by K'uchi-Wara's people.

- **qhapaq hucha** (Quechua): child who was sacrificed by the Inkas in a special ritual.

- **Qhapaq Raymi** (Quechua): Inka festival honoring the Sun; it was held around the December solstice.

- **qoa** (Quechua): malevolent spirit that took the form of a cat.

- **Quechua**: language spoken by the Inkas.

- **quinua** (Quechua): grain that is commonly grown in the Andean highlands.

- **q'iswa chaka** (Quechua): rope bridge.

- **Qulla-Suyu** (Quechua): southeastern quarter of the Inka Empire.

- **qutu** ("group" in Aymara): Pleiades; small constellation consisting of seven stars.

- **Santiago** (Spanish): capital of Chile; it is located in the central part of the country.

- **suruchi** ("antimony" in Quechua): altitude sickness.

- **tampu** (Quechua): lodging house situated along a royal road.

- **Tawantin-Suyu** ("land of the four quarters" in Quechua): Inka Empire.

- **Thupa Yapanqui** (Quechua): Inka king who reigned before K'uchi-Wara's time.

- **Titicaca**, Lake (Quechua): large body of water located on the high plateau between Peru and Bolivia.

- **Titi-Urqu** ("lead mountain" in Quechua): sacred peak near whose summit a boy was sacrificed.

- **tupu** (Quechua): measure of distance used for travelers on foot; it is equal to about 4 ½ miles.

- **uqa** (Quechua): tuber that is commonly grown in the Andean highlands.

- **vicuña** (Quechua): wild member of the camel family native to the Andes; it has extremely fine wool.

- **waqa** (Quechua): Andean idol or deity; any person, place, or thing with sacred power.

- **Wayna Qhapaq** (Quechua): Inka king who reigned in K'uchi-Wara's time.

- **Wila-Nayra** ("red eye" in Aymara): K'uchi-Wara's native community; it was named after a red pool located nearby.

- **Willka-kamayuq** (Quechua): state official in charge of the *waqas*.

- **Wira-Qucha** (Quechua): Inka creator god; after creating the world, he disappeared over the ocean.

- **yunka** (Aymara): temperate and forested land along the eastern slope of the Andes.

For More Information

For more information on the **Inkas**, see the following sources:

- D'Altroy, Terence, 2002. *The Incas*. Malden, MA: Blackwell Publishers Inc.

- Rowe, John, 1946. "Inca Culture at the Time of the Spanish Conquest." *Handbook of South American Indians*, bulletin 143, volume 2: 183-330. Edited by Julian Steward. Washington, DC: Smithsonian Institution.

For more information on the **Aymara**, see the following sources:

- Bastien, Joseph, 1985. *Mountain of the Condor: Metaphor and Ritual in an Andean Ayllu*. Prospect Heights, IL: Waveland Press, Inc.

- Tschopik, Harry, 1946. "The Aymara." *Handbook of South American Indians*, bulletin 143, volume 2: 501-573. Edited by Julian Steward. Washington, DC: Smithsonian Institution.

For more information on **human sacrifice** and **mountain worship** in the Andes, see the following sources:

- Besom, Thomas, 2009. *Of Summits and Sacrifice: An Ethnohistoric Study of Inka Religious Practices*. Austin, TX: University of Texas Press.

- Reinhard, Johan, 2005. *The Ice Maiden: Inca Mummies, Mountain Gods, and Sacred Sites in the Andes.* Washington, DC: National Geographic Society.

For more information on the **Mummy of Cerro El Plomo**, see the following sources:

- Besom, Thomas, 2013. *Inka Human Sacrifice and Mountain Worship: Strategies for Empire Unification.* Albuquerque, NM: University of New Mexico Press.

- Mostny, Grete (Editor), 1957. *La momia del cerro El Plomo.* Boletín del Museo Nacional de Historia Natural, tomo XXVII, número 1: 1-119. Santiago, Chile: Museo Nacional de Historia Natural.

For more information on **llama herding** in the Andes, see the following sources:

- Flannery, Kent, Joyce Marcus, and Robert Reynolds, 1989. *The Flocks of the Wamani: A Study of Llama Herders on the Punas of Ayacucho, Peru.* New York, NY: Academic Press, Inc.

- Flores-Ochoa, Jorge, 1979. *Pastoralists of the Andes: the Alpaca Herders of Paratía.* Translated by Ralph Bolton. Philadelphia, PA: Institute for the Study of Human Issues, Inc.

For more examples of the **illustrations** used in the book, see the following source:

- Guaman Poma de Ayala, Felipe, 1980 [1615] *El primer nueva corónica y buen gobierno.* Colección América nuestra, número 31. Transcribed and translated by Jorge Urioste. Mexico City, Mexico: Siglo Veintiuno Editores, S.A.

About the Illustrations

Felipe Guaman Poma de Ayala was a native of Peru. In the late 1500s and early 1600s, he wrote a thousand-page letter to the king of Spain. One reason for composing the letter was to protest the mistreatment of Peru's native people by the Spanish. To make his case, he compared life under the Inkas with daily existence in the Spanish colony. He illustrated the work with 398 pen-and-ink drawings. Whereas some of the drawings are clumsy, and others are more elegant, all are rich in detail.

The fourteen illustrations in *Child of the Snows* are based on Guaman Poma's images of the Inkas. In some cases, I have taken a drawing of his, have simplified it by eliminating extraneous elements, and have added details of my own. More often, though, I have taken several pictures, have cut them to pieces, and have recombined the pieces to make a collage.

The imagery in most of my illustrations is straightforward. The symbolism in the first and last pictures, however, requires some explanation. The former work shows a child buried within a mountain. Given that the Inka calendar was based on the appearance and disappearance of celestial bodies in the sky, the presence of the Old Sun, Moon, and Morning Star in the illustration signifies the passage of time. Throughout the book, K'uchi-Wara closely identifies with, and is associated by others with, the condor. So in the final picture, the emergence of this bird from the peak in which the boy has been entombed, represents the child's spirit leaving his body.

205

Notes from the Author

Child of the Snows is based on thirty-five years of research into the Inka practices of human sacrifice and mountain worship. I first became interested in the subjects while living in Santiago, Chile. I was in high school at the time. On Sunday afternoons, my father, knowing that I was interested in anthropology, would occasionally take me to the Museo Nacional de Historia Natural (MNHN), located in the Quinta Normal Park. There we would stroll down the long halls, looking at different exhibits. What I saw one day, though, while glancing into a refrigerated showcase, stopped me in my tracks. It was the frozen body of a little boy. He was curled up in a fetal position, and was surrounded by various items. A plaque next to the showcase referred to him as the *"Momia de Cerro El Plomo."* It went on to explain that the child had been offered up by the Inkas almost 500 years ago on Mount El Plomo, which at 5,430 meters (17,815 feet) is the highest peak visible from Santiago.

In graduate school, I began to study human sacrifice and mountain worship in earnest. Both my master's thesis and dissertation deal with these topics, as do two academic books that I later wrote. The second book, titled *Inka Human Sacrifice and Mountain Worship*, also discusses the Mummy of Cerro El Plomo.

Through my research, I learned that the child's well-preserved remains were discovered in February of 1954 by two treasure hunters: Gerardo Ríos and his friend, Jaime Ríos. Gerardo's uncle, Guillermo Chacón—a miner who had spent many years exploring El Plomo, and who had previously come upon three Inka *pircas* or stone structures near

207

the peak's summit—had told his nephew that he should dig in the largest structure. After finding and removing the body, the Ríoses hauled it down to the Cepo Valley at the foot of the mountain, where they re-buried it.

In March, the Ríoses and Chacón retrieved the child's remains—along with all the items that had been discovered with it—and took them to Santiago. Once there, Chacón met with Dr. Grete Mostny, head of the Anthropology Section of the MNHN, and showed her the archaeological materials. Mostny, immediately recognizing their importance, purchased them for the museum. She paid about $410.

Using information from my research, I wrote the first draft of *Child of the Snows* a decade ago. At the time, I was interested in the works of early American authors, including *The Scarlet Letter* by Nathaniel Hawthorne and *Moby Dick* by Herman Melville. I used parts of these books as patterns for scenes in my manuscript. I also was fascinated by the "magical realism" of certain Latin American writers, especially Isabel Allende of Chile. Her novels *The House of Spirits* and *Inés of My Soul* inspired particular chapters and characters in my manuscript.

Most authors will tell you that writing is a difficult process. The hardest part of it, however, is not the penning of the first draft, but rather all the revising that must subsequently take place. The initial manuscript for *Child of the Snows* was read by my parents, Don and Kay Besom, by my brother, also named Don, and by good friends, including Ann Williams. They offered thoughtful and insightful suggestions for bettering the novel. Later I took a graduate level creative writing course at Binghamton University (SUNY) with Professor Jaimee Wriston Colbert. As part of the course, I had to rewrite *Child of the Snows* based on the critiques of the professor and students, which made the manuscript considerably stronger. More recently, Anton Daughters and Betsy Delmonico, working on behalf of the Golden Antelope Press, gave me some useful advice for improving the novel still further. I am indebted to all these people for their help in making critical revisions.

Getting *Child of the Snows* published has been no easy task. I queried over 500 literary agents about representing the work, but was turned down by all of them. I also submitted the novel directly to numerous presses, most of which rejected it. I am glad, though, that it finally found a home with the Golden Antelope Press.